# MEAT CITY

## & other stories

## Jason M. Tucker

BLACK BED SHEET

Meat City (and Other Stories)
A Black Bed Sheet/Diverse Media Book
May 2010

Library of Congress Control Number: 2010927138

ISBN-10: 0-9842136-9-4
ISBN-13: 978-0-9842136-9-6

# Meat City

& Other Stories

**A Black Bed Sheet/Diverse Media Book**
Antelope, CA

# Also by Jason M. Tucker:

## *Anthologies*
## *& Contributions:*

*Darc Karnival*

*Horror Prodigies and Legends*

*Northern Haunts*

*The Rare Anthology*

●

## DEDICATION

For Adrianna and Kayla: You two are greatest and most understanding daughters in the world

For Erin and Shaun: You are some of the greatest friends a person could ever find, friends who were there when no one else was

For Carrie and Tricia: Thanks making sure I don't "borrow" golf carts and boats, for illuminating the fate of most of my missing clothing, and for making sure that my ravenous stupidity is (slightly) reined in when there is a full moon and vodka present, and, well, for dealing with my escapades and misadventures over many years

For Mom: Thank you for passing on a love of stories

I love you all

●

# Contents

# Meat City

## & Other Stories

Jason M. Tucker

# BAD GIRL

## 1.

"Sometimes the dead whisper," said Angie, her voice a choked whisper. "I see them." With tears flooding her eyes, she looked over the support group. She panned from one face to another, then another. The newest members, the ones still strung out, gave her nothing but hollow looks filled with their own pain. The ones that knew her, peers that had been in the Center for awhile, cried along with her.

"Angie, honey, you don't have to do this if you're not ready. . . ." said Victoria, the group's counselor. She had moved from her usual spot along the faded blue walls and drifted to Angie's side, placed a hand gently on her shoulder. "You still need time."

Angie nodded. She thought she could do it, but when she had started to talk about her children, the pain was too great. There were still things that she couldn't face herself. How could she expect anyone else to understand? She couldn't tell them the truth.

"Trisha," Victoria said, "could you take her to her room?"

Trisha, a slender black woman who had been in the Center almost as long as Angie had, took her by the hand. Angie hurried out of the small and suddenly hot room, averting her eyes from everyone's gaze.

When they finally reached Angie's room, Trisha spoke. "You feeling okay?"

"Sure," Angie lied, wiping away tears with the back of her hand. She would never feel okay. Angie thought that checking herself into the Center to get clean and face her past would help her. She was wrong, and she'd never felt that more than now.

"You said that you see them . . . what did you mean by that?" Trisha asked.

"Nothing," Angie said. "Ramblings of an ex-addict, that's all."

"No such thing as an ex-addict," Trisha said. "Come on, we've known each other for near six months now. You trust me, don't you?"

Angie nodded and opened the door. She slipped inside and hesitated before inviting Trisha into the small room. "If I tell you, you're just going to think I'm nuts."

"You've never met my family. No matter how wacko you think you are, you don't have anything on them."

Angie tried to smile but couldn't find one.

"Okay, lay it on me," Angie said. "You might feel better once you let it out. We've all done things we aren't proud of, thought some crazy things. You're not alone."

"I see them sometimes. Just out of the corners of my eyes, but I know they're watching me." It was coming out and it felt like shit. She kept her head down so she didn't have to see Trisha's face. Her heart hammered and her vision blurred. She couldn't believe she was going to tell someone. God, she shouldn't say

2

anything. Her mouth didn't listen to her head though. "I hear them too, whispering. I hear them more now that I'm clean."

"Who are you talking about?"

"My children," Angie said, looking up at Trisha.

Trisha smiled wide. "I don't think you're crazy, and that isn't anything to be scared of. It's just the spirits coming back to look at their momma, to watch over her."

"I don't like it," Angie said. "I can't stand it, it doesn't feel good, and it doesn't feel right. They shouldn't be here."

There was more. Angie could not tell Trisha about *that* though.

"Spirits can come back to watch the ones they love," Trisha said. "My grandmother told me that, and I believe that too."

Trisha wondered what happened if the dead didn't love though. "They tell me I'm a bad girl."

"No, they wouldn't –" Trisha began, but Angie cut her off.

"You don't know," Angie said.

"You checked yourself into this place to get help," Trisha said. "The only thing I did was show you the way here. You aren't bad; you were just mixed up with some bad stuff and now you're working to get better."

"No," Angie said.

"Look," Trisha said, pointing to a drawing on the wall. The drawing, done by a child's unsteady hand, contained a picture of a little girl and boy standing on a green hill beneath a yellow spiral sun. In the lower left hand corner there was a blue handprint. "Your kids did that for you, huh?"

"Yes," she said, swallowing her own self-loathing. "Samantha drew the picture and Kyle put his little hand print on it. It was for my birthday two years ago."

"You see," Trisha said, "they love you."

*They are dead because of me*, she thought. "I'm going to get some sleep."

"Okay sweetie, I'll see you later."

## 2.

Sleep would not come, she knew, no matter how long she stared at the white ceiling and counted. In each of the fifteen tiles was one-hundred and twenty-three tiny holes; they reminded her of needle tracks that once ran along her arms.

The dinner bell rang, but she stayed in bed beneath her gray wool blanket. At least in her room she didn't have to look at the others. Some of them shook because they needed a fix so badly, while others talked to themselves. All of them reminded her of what she was. Even the worst of them had never done anything half as bad as she had, of that she was certain.

She had been clean for almost six months. Not a drop of liquor or heroin-filled needle had come even close to her. Physically, she felt wonderful. Without the drug and booze to cloud her vision, she could remember the past though. The past was a place she could not bear.

She remembered her children; Samantha was six and Kyle had just turned four when they died. She had no idea where the father was; he vanished after Kyle's birth. That was about the time Angie remembered starting to drink heavily. Time was a blur then: fights with her parents, spending her money on booze and later heroin, and then her blazing ride to a self-annihilation. She had hated everything back then, hated herself, her parents, and even her children.

Then the offer that snatched her last bit of humanity came. Both of her children for a thousand dollars. She could not remember the face of the man that gave her the cash nor his name. None of it even seemed real at the time. Not that it mattered, because the only thing that she really remembered was that it kept her in drugs for a little while.

When the police came to tell her that her babies had been found with slit throats, floating face down in a stagnant pond, she panicked. She told them that they someone took them but she was too strung out to report it. They never found the killer, and she'd had solid alibis of where she was. She couldn't even remember caring.

Trisha found her not long after and convinced her to come to the Center, a place where she could deal with her problems, check in and out when she wanted, and they even helped her find a part time job to help her on the road to self-sufficiency. It took some convincing, but she finally went. It was a different kind of rehab but it had worked for quite a few people.

It cleaned her up, certainly. She was ready for that. At least she thought she was ready. Being clean untied painful memories and let them claw their way to her mind's surface. All that anyone in Center knew about her children was that they died in an accident.

"One hundred-eighteen," she whispered to the holes on the ceiling. "One hundred-nineteen. . . ."

## 3.

Angie had not even realized that she was tired, much less tired enough to have fallen asleep. The room was dark, lit only by the orange streetlight that filtered in through the windows.

She squinted through the gloom so she could read the dull green numbers on her digital alarm clock. It was well after eleven, already long past lights out.

A growl followed by a sharp pinch in her stomach reminded her that she had missed dinner. Mrs. Nguyen, the residential cook, did not like anyone messing up her kitchen after hours. Still, she could head down to the lobby and grab a candy bar and a soda to hold her until morning.

The building was silent, except for the almost imperceptible hum of the candy and soda machines in the lobby. Angie slid coin after coin into the machine, which ate them greedily. She pushed the bright button marked Orange.

"I like grape soda," a voice, a tiny waif of a voice, said.

Angie spun around, her eyes wide like a deer that knows it's caught in the sights of a hunter's rifle.

Trisha's slender form blocked the hallway. "I said I knew I'd catch you down here."

"You said you liked grape soda."

"I hate grape," said Trisha.

Angie shook her head. "I guess I heard wrong. Still waking up."

She knew what she had heard. She also knew Trisha hadn't said it. The voice had sounded like Kyle.

"Well, I saved you a plate of dinner. Meatloaf and mashed potatoes, Mrs. Nguyen's version of M&Ms."

## 4.

Two days later Angie got a good look at her dead son's face in the mirror. She had just finished showering, stepped out into the steam-filled room and saw, only for a second, her boy's face, same dark eyes and blond hair, the crooked nose; there was a dark line at his neck where a knife had sliced him open. Then it was gone.

## 5.

"I think I'm going crazy," she told Trisha later that afternoon. "It's not right that I see them like this. I don't know why it's happening." She did know. They were coming back to remind her, to torment her for the rest of her days. She knew she deserved it.

"Why do you think they want to hurt you?"

Angie shrugged.

"Out with it, girl."

Breathing deeply, regretting the words as they left her mouth, she began. "My children didn't die in a car accident . . . ."

There, in the solarium, it came out, most of it in muted whispers and sobs. When she was finally done, she looked into Trisha's eyes for comfort, but there was none. Only hatred resided in the woman's dark orbs.

"I can't believe you did that to your babies," were the only words to come out of her mouth. She stood and walked briskly away.

## 6.

"Mommy, wake up." It was her daughter this time, tearing Angie from an uneasy sleep into a waking nightmare. When she finally dared open her eyes, her daughter was not there.

Outside a cold rain had started; she could hear it beat against the roof, could feel the chill seep in through the tiny cracks in the floor. The chill seemed to creep along the floor and up the bed sheet to her body, where it entered her pores and froze her veins. They were aching dully, and she knew more pain would be coming. This was the first time in a long time that she wanted heroin. It could make things better, even if it was just for a little while.

"And it takes away the memories," she whispered to the darkness.

"Be a good girl, Mommy," Kyle's phantom voice commanded.

Angie covered her ears, afraid to listen, however sound the advice might be. She stood and dressed and then, paying no more attention to the small voices that pleaded with her to stay, walked away.

## 7.

Finding a dealer on East San Diego streets was easy, even in the rain. Convincing him to trade the dope for a gold necklace and a blowjob was not. Eventually he relented, tired of her hounding him, and gave it to her. It wasn't a lot, but it might be enough to take her away from reality, at least for a while.

## 8.

"Angie, honey," Trisha said, pushing open the door to her room. "We should talk about what you told me. I . . ." Trisha stood silent in the room, staring at the mess on the floor.

Angie was there, naked on the cold bare floor. Her eyes were wide open, glazed over and dead. A syringe jutted out of her arm. On her stomach was a drawing of a boy and girl on a hill, a nearly exact replica of the one that hung on her wall, except that here the spiral sun was crimson and the clouds were dripping red. A tiny bloodied handprint decorated Angie's bare hipbone.

"Mommy was a bad girl," a voice whispered in Trisha's ear. She could feel small, cold hands tugging at her flower print dress. "Are you a bad girl, too?"

# CITY OF A MILLION GODS

## 1.

Christian Shaw stood beneath the Collier Hotel's green awning and stared out at the drab leaking sky that mirrored the dull color of the monolithic buildings. The thick traffic, with every other car seeming to be a painfully bright yellow taxi, crawled past with aching slowness. He looked at his watch and wondered where Joseph could be with their rented Ford Taurus. After all, the parking garage was just around the corner.

His time in New York measured less than a week, and each day had been just as rainy and miserable. That aspect was not much different from his native Liverpool. Still, he was determined not to let weather ruin his vacation. Joseph and he had visited museums and seen a Broadway show. They even stood in the pouring rain to see Strawberry Fields in Central Park.

A few moments and several yellow taxis later, Joseph pulled alongside the curb and Christian braved the short expanse from awning to car. He got in and shook the rain from his hair.

"Watch where you're spraying that," Joseph said, shielding his face from the watery onslaught as he pulled into the dense traffic. Christian detected

10

irritation in his voice, and he knew what was coming next. It had been Joseph's mantra the past few days.

Joseph sighed. "Why come to this rotten city to get rained on? I could've stayed in bloody London if I wanted a shower every time I stepped outside. You know we should have gone to California. Los Angeles or San Diego, they're always sunny and warm. And who the fuck rents a car in New York?"

"We could always stay at the hotel," Christian said with a smile. He watched as the anger faded from Joseph's face and the corners of his mouth lifted. Good. The last thing he wanted now was for Joseph to be in a foul mood.

"I've already spent an hour getting the car," he said, "and I'm not going to put it back now. So there's no need to get snippy, we'll go on your little tunnel excursion."

The clash of cultures in New York City had always fascinated Christian. More faiths, desires, and peoples congregated there than London and Paris combined, and while known for its violence, the city still stood strong.

He and Joseph were having a conversation on just that topic the previous night, while sipping cappuccino in a posh, dimly lit coffee house. It was there that they met Samuel and Lily, a young couple dressed from head to toe in black. The couple had obviously been listening in on the discourse because Samuel had leaned over and said, "This is the city of a million gods."

He was a short, wiry figure with a shaved head and red lenses in his square-framed glasses.

"And how many have you tasted?" Joseph had asked, with the usual amount of cynicism in his voice. "Fickle folk in New York and all."

Lily, with cardinal lips and alabaster skin that looked as delicate as the petals of her namesake, had answered. She pushed her dark hair out of her eyes. "Enough to know that there is one true god, and he's not the one you worship."

"How do you know what god we worship?" Christian said, knowing that he would enjoy the ensuing conversation. Photography was his profession, but world mythology and theology were his hobbies. He also knew that Joseph, a professional rugby player, would unfortunately be bored.

"You've never met our god," Samuel said with a certain degree of confidence. A warm smile played brightly across his face. "Although I'm sure you know some of his faces."

"Our loss," Joseph said, and downed the last of his cappuccino.

"Tell us about your god, about your religion," Christian had urged, pretending he did not see the look of disgust Joseph had given him.

"There is too much to tell," Lily said.

"But we could show you. Tomorrow," Samuel had said. After giving directions to what Samuel had called the Tunnel of Enlightenment, he quickly turned the conversation to another topic, which instantly brightened Joseph's mood. Samuel, it seemed, was a rugby fan and had recognized Joseph. That had stroked Joseph's ego, appeasing him at least for the night.

The rest of the evening had gone by smoothly, with Samuel and Joseph discussing sports and why warm ale was better than cold, while Christian and Lily

12

talked about photography and the underground music scene of New York and London.

## 2.

"This is it? You must be joking," said Joseph, when he stepped out of the car and looked upon what was supposed to be the Tunnel of Enlightenment's entrance. Samuel and Lily, dressed in jeans and dirty sweatshirts, stood smiling in front of a large storm drain opening. "There's something wrong here."

Christian shook his head, "You always think the worst about people."

"This is New York City. They are probably going to rob us and kill us. That's just what my vacation needs to make it perfect, the full New York experience." Joseph did not move from beside the vehicle. "I bet they're part of a cult."

"All religions were once cults," Christian said. "To become a full-fledged religion, all you need are a few years, some followers, and a sprinkling of zealots to keep it interesting."

"You aren't really thinking of going beneath the city with them, are you?" Joseph's face scrunched. "Don't be a dolt."

Christian loved Joseph's sense of responsibility and the way he thought through everything. It was the perfect complement to Christian's flightiness. However, the big rugby player just did not have a sense of adventure, and he could be downright venomous. Just getting him to leave London was a major feat.

"I want to go. You know how I love this stuff."

"Love what," Joseph muttered, "getting killed or driving me insane?"

"The last one," Christian said, as he turned his back and started toward Samuel and Lily. "Who knows," he continued, patting his camera bag, "I might even get to take some interesting pictures to sell, pay for the whole trip."

Christian grinned when he heard Joseph huff and slam the car door shut. He soon heard Joseph hurrying toward him. "I suppose I can't just let you go alone to get brainwashed or killed or whatnot. That wouldn't be very gentlemanly."

Lily waved them forward.

"I didn't think you two would actually show up," Samuel said, as he and Lily turned to enter the tunnel. They each turned on a flashlight. "Most people fear the truth."

"I knew you would come," Lily said, smiling at Christian. "I felt it last night, when we first met."

"That's lovely," said Joseph, "she could *feel* you." Christian ignored him.

Lily continued. "You are a scholar at heart, and I can tell that you truly desire enlightenment."

True enough, he thought, at least when it came to the subjects of religion and myth. The possibility of discovering a new urban religion was a titillating thought. Perhaps even write a book on the subject, he mused, as they passed into the tunnel's darkness.

The storm drain's mouth was garbage strewn and stank of urine. Amidst the refuse Samuel stood, pulling at an old ice chest. When he – along with Joseph's help – had gotten the thing out of the way, Christian could see a small hole. The roughly hewn circle was barely large enough for a man of Joseph's size to squeeze through.

"This is ridiculous!" Joseph threw his hands up in the air. Then he pointed at the hole. "You expect us to go through there?"

Christian could see Samuel grinning in the flashlight's glow. "I thought men like you were accustomed to fitting into tight little holes."

"Fuck you," Joseph said, the hint of a growl in his voice. "I'm getting out of this fucking tunnel." Even in the darkness, Christian could feel Joseph's eyes upon him. "Are you coming?"

"I just want to see," Christian said.

"Right, you fucking dolt," Joseph said, spinning around and heading toward the entrance. "I'll be in the car. If you aren't back soon, you can walk to the Collier."

He started to go after Joseph, but he felt a soft hand light upon his shoulder. It was Lily, gently holding him back. "I need him," Christian said, looking after his partner.

"You don't," she said.

"You don't understand –"

"Don't worry," she whispered, "he'll be there for you when we're done, and if he's not then he does not deserve you. And he can serve another purpose."

She was right, he knew. Joseph was a wonderful man, but he was short of temper and his mind was small. It was just his nature. There had never been any real violence in the relationship, but there were plenty of times when Joseph would be gone for days at a time doing God knew what. Now, Christian thought with a slight perverse satisfaction, it was time Joseph got the chance to worry.

Christian entered the hole after Samuel and found that after a few feet of wriggling the aperture widened and it was possible to crawl along on hands and knees. Soon, the hole opened into a large cavity that appeared to have been carved by human hands. The flashlights could only illuminate part of the cavern, so he could not tell how extensive the place really was.

"This is where you worship?" Christian had a sinking feeling that perhaps Joseph had been right. Here, in the shadows, there could be any number of people waiting to take his money or his life.

"Not here," Samuel said. "We still have a ways to go."

"There," Lily said, pointing the beam of her light toward a wooden ladder that looked ancient and half-rotted. "We go down the ladder."

"Tell me about your god," Christian said, as they neared the ladder. He glanced nervously at the shadows, expecting to see grinning faces and switchblades; there was nothing but shadows.

"He is an amalgamation of deities and antiquated faiths," Samuel said when he was halfway down the rickety ladder. The flashlight, which was tucked into his belt and shining upward, gave his face an eerie glow. "Created by the city and the memories of its people."

Lily continued. "No one religion is completely right, you see. They all have bits and pieces that are factual, like the Flood. And evil, all religions acknowledge the presence of overpowering evil."

"From my studies," Christian said, "many religions exaggerated the tales of evil things that inhabited the worlds of flesh and spirit as a way to impose order, from the myths of the Romans to Christianity."

16

"Myths?"

"Well, they are all just myths, aren't they? At least until we die and find out for sure, it's all a myth. Imagine the afterlife is actually Valhalla! The bloody Vikings were right!" He smiled, though in the low light he was sure she couldn't see.

Lily urged Christian to go down the ladder next.

Each rung of the ladder was slippery and covered in some kind of slime, and he wished that he had worn shoes that were more sensible. He couldn't be too upset with himself, however, because when he had dressed that morning, he had no idea where the day would take him. When he reached the bottom of the ladder, which was about four meters high, Samuel showed him a passage that had been shored up with wooden beams. "Through there is enlightenment," Samuel whispered. "You will experience wonders you never thought possible."

Lily was beside them now, an arm draped over Samuel's shoulder. "Go ahead," she said. Her voice was silky.

"This is nothing like I thought it would be," Christian said, laughing nervously. "You see, I thought it would be more like a church meeting group. You know, with warm apple cider and cake."

"Leaving is not an option," Samuel said, stepping in front of the ladder with Lily.

"I see," Christian replied, shrugging. More than being robbed, he dreaded the look of *'I told you so'* that he knew Joseph would give him. "Is it money that you want? I'll give you whatever I have."

"We don't care about money," Samuel said, as though he were above such a petty thing as wealth. "Just go and meet our god, learn true faith."

Christian was not as good a judge of people as Joseph was, but he could see malice in their eyes and the glint of a long blade held in Samuel's hand. Unless he wanted a knife in the stomach, he knew he would have to do as they asked. "Can I at least have a light?"

Along the walls of the passage were etched symbols and figures depicting ancient gods and demons. Some of them he recognized from books he had read, but others he had never seen, either something new or something very old. The flashlight's incandescence made the figures appear as though they were moving, following him along the wet and musty corridor.

He walked for what seemed like an eon, marveling at the images on the wall, when he saw a soft light begin to glow in the distance. As he neared the light source at the passage's end, he became aware of a powerful stench, as though something was rotting.

He knew the smell. It was putrefying flesh, the same smell that had accosted him several years before at his flat in the East End. His elderly neighbor, Mr. Hobbes, had died in May and was not discovered until the middle of a hot July. But the stench that wafted from the edge of the corridor was far more powerful.

The part of him that thought rationally told him to turn around, to run, to use the flash on his camera to blind Samuel and Lily and to run past them. Something kept him from turning and running, though. He supposed it was curiosity, simply the need to find out just what it was that waited for him. Perhaps they were telling the truth; maybe it was some new god and enlightenment as far fetched as that seemed. Whatever was there, it seemed to be drawing him forward.

18

When he reached the end of the hallway he had to squint to see inside the next room, for the light had become incredibly bright. When his eyes finally adjusted, he saw heaps of skeletons and rotting corpses. There must have been a hundred bodies, he guessed. Maybe more.

Atop the heap sat a strange, wizened creature that, when Christian looked upon it, began to sing a melancholy song in a voice barely above a whisper. It was naked, and its wrinkled skin was a mottled gray. A dark mane ran from head to serpentine tail. Coarse bristles covered each of its four arms. The creature's face was partially elongated, giving it the appearance of some sort of canine or perhaps even Anubis, but the eyes . . . the eyes were far more than human, far more intelligent and soulful. There was wisdom in those eyes, but there was also darkness.

The thing stood on its two spindly legs and began to slowly dance amongst the bones, sending them tumbling down the bone mountain. Still, it sang the song, and the melody seemed to be reaching into Christian's mind, exchanging thoughts with him, sharing histories. Searching him as the creature told of itself.

Its name was incomprehensible, but when translated it roughly meant the Eternal Bone Dancer, or He Who Wallows Among the Dead. Christian could tell that great sadness and anger pervaded the once proud creature.

Bone Dancer was created from the remains of the dead gods, those who had fallen out of favor, ancient gods of the harvest and wine and of plague, and a million such things. He was pieces of Zeus and Odin and Apollo, gods who were once champions of the heavens. They only existed within him now. In this, the Age of Lust and Desire, he was nothing when compared to the great gods known as Greed, Power, and Fame.

And, as humiliating as it was, he had become mere flesh, and as such he was prey to the sins of the flesh. He needed sex and food, pleasure and entertainment. Thus, Christian thought, the heap of bones.

The ones outside, Samuel and Lily, were two of his most faithful followers, constantly recruiting new believers, ones who searched for enlightenment. The flock was small now. With enough followers, he could again ascend from his pit and take back the earth and the heavens. Bone Dancer reasoned that if Christ could resurrect and arise then it could happen to him too.

*Do you seek enlightenment*? It sang in a plethora of voices.

Christian nodded, knowing that Bone Dancer already knew his greatest desires, his deepest fears. They had exchanged secrets and truths.

Bone Dancer leapt off the pile of bones and came within inches of him. Christian could smell the putrid human meat on his breath, but he was not afraid. He leaned forward and kissed Christian on the lips. The god's kiss was exhilarating; it was like nothing he had ever felt before. There were sweetness, history, and *reality* in the touch.

## 3.

"Have you found enlightenment?" Lily asked when he emerged from the passage.

"Of course he has. He would be dead if he hadn't." Samuel was smiling broadly. "You know the work we must do."

Christian nodded dully. He was still numb from the god's touch. "I know what to do. He needs disciples, and he needs food. We will be the apostles and scribes in his Ascension."

"About your friend," Lily said, "what will he think?"

Christian shrugged absently. He had sifted through a hundred different religions, had more than his share of lovers, and in all his life he had never found anything that made him truly happy, that made him believe.

Until now.

Joseph would understand. He had to because everything was finally clear and the world made sense, albeit a twisted sense. This was what life meant. If Joseph didn't understand . . . well, Lily said he could serve another purpose. After all, the Bone Dancer needed to be entertained and He needed to eat.

# COVENTRY GREENS

Until I was twelve years old, I lived in the quiet little town of Coventry and spent most weekends hanging out with Hooper Johns, my best friend.

I'll never forget what I did to him.

Hooper came over to the house on a cold Saturday afternoon in October. Being twelve, we soon found ourselves bored. We weren't at the age yet where we thought chasing girls or sneaking booze would be any fun, so instead we decided to see if we could find the Greenies.

Everyone had tales about the Greenies, inbred folk from the backcountry. People said they were deformed and their skin was green like a witch. Stories like that were gold for kids our age.

Anyway, Hooper and me grabbed our bikes and told my mother we were heading into town to grab some pizza at Marco Polo's. Instead, we pedaled in the opposite direction and down Harkney Hill Road until we finally came to a little dirt road that led towards Johnson Pond.

The road became a footpath so we ditched our bikes. Hooper – *poor Hooper* – said it was getting dark

22

and that we should just forget it. I told him he was a pussy – just about the worst thing one twelve-year-old boy could call another. His shoulders slumped and he nodded.

We walked another quarter mile into the woods until the trail vanished among the weeds and briars.

Then we heard it, a high-pitched whooping sound. I hoped that maybe it was a loon – they make some awful noises – but deep down Hooper and I knew it wasn't birds.

We turned to leave and saw one of them about fifty yards away. It darted into the trees. The remaining sunlight bounced of its twisted, deep green flesh.

Another whoop erupted from the woods behind us, then two more from the front. The Greenies were hunting.

Well, Hooper must have lost it because he took off running and screaming, arms flailing. I did the same. The trail became a blur, and I was strangely aware I had to piss. Then something smashed into the side of my head and I hit the ground hard.

When I awoke, it took a moment for the scene to focus. I was in the corner of what looked and smelled like a slaughter shack, like the kind where my father used to butcher deer. The only light came from lanterns hanging from the ceiling. Dried blood spattered the walls.

I heard Hooper whimpering and saw him splayed out on a wooden table. Two Greenies pinned him down as he writhed and tried to get away. Another Greenie, a woman, stood over him. She was chanting unintelligibly and holding something bright green that wriggled in her hand. It looked like a giant worm or grub, one end filled with gnashing teeth.

The woman lowered the worm-thing toward Hooper, and it started to burrow its way inside through his *Thundercats* t-shirt and into his chest. He started screaming. I must have started screaming too because the Greenies turned toward me. Their eyes were pure white. One let go of Hooper and scrambled toward me. I lashed out with a kick that caught his deformed face and stunned him.

Then I was up and running. Screaming, I ran past the other Greenies and out of the shack. I left Hooper, but I caught his frightened eyes on the way out. I never stopped; I never looked back. I left my best friend there with those things and I never forgave myself.

***

They never found Hooper, and by the time they got to the slaughter shack, the Greenies were gone, probably heading deeper into the wilderness. They searched for months and found nothing. We moved away to Warren the next summer.

I did see Hooper again though. It was just last week, when I took the boys out fishing on Black Pond.

Hooper hid in the bushes across the pond eyeing me. He was still wearing his *Thundercats* t-shirt, now faded, torn, and many sizes too small. His limbs were twisted and his skin was green. His eyes were pure white and angry.

I got a bad feeling I might see him again soon.

# GOD OF WORMS

## 1.

Mark's voice was almost gone. His throat and lungs were raw from screaming, but he continued calling his brother's name. Despite being beneath the forest canopy, the sound of the driving rain was deafening.

He tried to focus his eyes in the dim, rain-drenched forest but could see little beyond the tiny cone of light that his flashlight emitted. In the distance, he would catch the occasional flash of another searcher's light, a pinprick of brightness in the dark void.

The scent of evergreen was thick, but an underlying smell of decay was also present. Dead needles and leaves had their own special, rotten smell, a scent Mark detested.

"Simon," Mark called, cupping one hand around his mouth. He uttered a silent prayer to a God he hoped was listening.

He knew it was his fault Simon was gone. Mark had spent the better part of his thirty years looking out for his sweet and simple-minded older brother and he'd done as good a job of it as anyone could ask.

He spent every part of his life caring for Simon – he had refused promotions and better jobs that would've taken up more of his time, girlfriends that would've done the same. He pushed away everything that a normal life entailed. But everything could be undone in a heartbeat.

Simon loved the trees behind Mark's house and would spend hours in the backyard watching the birds and trying to photograph them with the digital camera Mark bought for him two Christmases earlier.

He would fill entire photo albums and look at the pictures each day. Simon had a story that went along with every single one of the pictures.

Thinking of those bird photos – although in truth, many of the photos were simply skewed snapshots of brush and trees that Simon thought *might* have birds in them – drove Mark mad. How was he to know that today Simon would just walk into the woods and disappear? He had never done anything like that in the past. He'd always stayed just at the edge of the woods. Who could know?

"Simon!" he screamed again and his voice broke. Off to his left, Mark heard several voices shouting in unison. He could barely make out what they were saying over the rain, but he was sure they were calling his name. Maybe they found Simon.

Mark took off running through the rain-slicked forest, navigating the thick carpet of pine needles and twigs as carefully as he could. In the distance, he could see more of those pinpoints of light gathering. They had found something. *Please let him be okay*, Mark thought.

It seemed to take forever to reach those flashlights but when he finally did, he saw Simon. A searcher, one of the men hastily gathered from the diner down in

Silver Point by the Sheriff, had already wrapped a blanket around his brother's hunched form.

"Hey," Simon said. "Sorry." His head was down, eyes focused on the ground. It was characteristic of the manner in which he always spoke. One hand fiddled with his camera, the other scratched at his neck. He looked pale and frightened, and somehow he looked smaller than Mark remembered.

Mark hugged Simon and could feel him shaking. "It's okay. Don't worry."

"It wasn't a good time," said Simon, his head and eyes lifting slightly. The eyes held the same dull glaze they always did. "I didn't have fun. I didn't see any birds tonight and now I itch."

"We gotta get you checked out at the hospital, okay? Make sure everything's okay with you," Mark said.

Simon shrugged. "I don't know. I really should stay. He wants me to stay. Will they fix my itch? I don't think they can. The worms are eating me."

"They will fix you up real good. You can see Big Jim," Mark said, as he and the half dozen or so volunteers began making their way out of the forest and back up to the backyard and the driveway beyond. Simon tried to look over his shoulder into the dark woods occasionally, but Mark kept him walking steadily forward.

The wind howled and the rain whipped into Mark's face and just as he was buckling Simon into the car, he thought he heard a voice riding the elements, a voice that called to Simon. He looked quickly around and saw the taillights of everyone else heading past his house and down the gravel driveway. There was no one around who could have said anything.

## 2.

Caldwell Hospital was just a short drive from Mark's house, down through the small town of Silver Point and along Route 28 to the somewhat larger town of North Caldwell. The rain, however, made the drive to the old three-story brick building last nearly forty minutes.

By the time they arrived, James "Big Jim" Haddock, the doctor who had taken care of Simon's every ailment over the past twenty-eight years, was waiting outside for them with an umbrella and a concerned smile. The umbrella looked small in his massive hands.

Mark gave Jim a wave. Simon continued to lean his head against the window and mutter about how he shouldn't have gone into the woods.

Mark got out of the car and hurried round to the passenger side where Jim waited with the umbrella.

"As soon as I got off the phone with you, I took the liberty of setting up a room for Simon to stay in tonight," Jim said.

"Thanks. I think he's okay, but he's got a bit of an itch. The whole way here I had to keep telling him to stop scratching."

"He might've tangled with some poison oak or gotten into some nettles. I'll give him a good look over and see how he's doing," Jim said, as he reached for the car door handle and opened it.

"Big Jim," Simon said, glancing upward.

"I hear you had quite an adventure today. Gave your brother a bit of a scare, huh?"

28

Simon shrugged. "Someone said my name. I thought it might be a bird, so I went and looked. It wasn't a bird, not at all."

"Let's get you inside," Mark said. He reached out a hand and waited for Simon to take it.

"You can't fix me," Simon said. He raised his hands as if he was showing them to Mark and Jim. They were bloody from where he had scratched himself raw. "I got the worms now and no one can fix me. The man from the woods told me so."

## 3.

Simon lay flat beneath the thin covers on his hospital bed and raised his bandaged hands above his face so he could look at them. "They still itch. Everything itches. Worms are everywhere inside."

Mark had been watching Simon for the past twenty minutes, ever since Jim bandaged his hands and drew blood to send to the lab. Simon had been complaining about his hands and talking about the supposed man in the woods the whole time.

Mark didn't know what to think. Had Simon really seen someone down in the woods? Jim seemed to think that Simon imagined it as he imagined birds in so many of his photos of empty bushes. Jim said that they should ignore the talk. The more Simon rambled on about the strange man, however, the more Mark started to think that maybe there had been someone in the woods, and that maybe someone had hurt his brother.

"Tell me about the man down in the woods," Mark said, shifting his weight in the uncomfortable chair. The room was icy and the scent of antiseptics made him nauseous. He equated the smell with his mother's death at the hospital years before when the cancer finally took her. He hated the thought of spending the whole night in the hospital, but he wasn't about to leave his brother alone.

"Probably shouldn't say anything more about him," said Simon. "He knows lots of things, even things in my head. I shouldn't tell you more."

"Why?" Mark shifted in his seat.

"He said not to," said Simon. His voice had softened to nearly a whisper.

"You know you can tell me anything. We talked about that. I can take care of anything that bothers you."

"The man in the woods said I'm better off with him, that I'm bad for you. He said mom died because I was dumb and I broke her heart."

"That's not true, Simon. You know that."

Simon was quiet for a moment "The God of Worms. He's hungry. Part of him is inside me now. He knows how to get me. His worms put things in my head. I think he wants more than just me. He's very hungry."

"You've had a crazy day, bro. You'll feel better after you get some sleep."

"I wish those people didn't find me. It would have been better. Now you know about the worms too. They mush me up inside so he can eat me, and make me part of him. And then he says we're going to make more."

"Simon . . . ."

"He's on my camera if you want to see him." Simon reached toward the stand next to the bed and used a bandaged hand to nudge his camera toward Mark. "Look. Twelve megapixels."

Mark took the digital camera but didn't turn it on. He didn't want to look through the pictures, not just yet.

The door opened and Mark flinched, nearly dropping the camera. Simon's stories were getting to him.

It was just Jim. The doctor smiled down at Simon. "How's that itching? Is the cream working?"

"Worms, Big Jim, but not like the ones that ate Mom when she went in the ground," Simon said. "Cream can't help. Fish can't either."

Jim turned his head toward Mark. "Still going on about the worms?"

Mark nodded and then stood up. "I think I'm going to step outside and get some fresh air. Why don't you come with me, Jim? Please."

"It's still raining."

"Please." Mark put a hand on Jim's shoulder and tried to usher him toward the door.

"Uh . . . sure," Jim said.

They stepped outside into the parking area at the rear of the hospital. He told Jim about the things Simon was saying, things that weren't characteristic of him. He didn't know what could have affected his brother so much.

Jim, the only smoking doctor Mark had ever met, lit a cigarette and took a deep puff. He ran a hand through his gray hair and shrugged. "You know as well as I do that Simon likes repetition. He likes his days to be the same. Get up, get dressed, eat cereal, and take pictures of birds. Today was a shock to him, that's all. He'll be right in a day or so, once he gets back to his routine."

"I hope so," Mark said. "What if he did see someone in the woods though?"

"You mean some asshole that just wanted to mess with him? I suppose that's possible," Jim said. "The chance of him just running into somebody in the woods that wanted to play a practical joke is pretty slim though, don't you think?"

"I don't know," Mark said. It wouldn't be the first time. Mark learned how to fight from spending the better part of his youth defending his older brother from inbred yokels and bullies determined to prove their own stupidity. Mark carried scars, badges of honor in his brother's defense.

He turned on the camera and he and Jim huddled together to look at the pictures on the small LCD screen. The first few pictures were as Mark had suspected. There was a shot of a bush, a close up of some papery birch bark, and a very good photo of a northern shrike in mid-flight. The sky in the next picture was darker and starting to fill with clouds as the storm rolled through. The following photo was deep in the woods, and half-hidden behind the thick trunk of a hemlock was what appeared to be a blurry figure.

"There," said Jim, jabbing a finger at the screen. "That looks a bit like a person. Maybe Simon's right, maybe there was someone out there."

Mark advanced the camera to the next picture. There, standing in the center of a small grove, was a thing no one would ever mistake for a man.

It was man-shaped, certainly, but that was where the similarities ended. The thing was the color of wet sand and it was naked. The bulbous head had no eyes, no nose, but a circular mouth full of what looked like very sharp teeth. The skin of the thing looked pockmarked from afar but when Mark zoomed in on the picture, he could see what looked to be worms in many of the tiny holes. He could see other worms clinging elsewhere on the thing's body.

"No," Jim said. He backed away from the camera, shaking his head. He flicked the remainder of his cigarette into a puddle. "No. That doesn't exist. Some kind of joke."

Mark turned off the camera and shoved it into his coat pocket with trembling hands. What Mark believed didn't matter anymore. He'd seen what was on the camera, felt it rip through his own sanity the moment he laid eyes on it. Poor Simon had seen it in the flesh.

Jim's eyes were big, wild. Gone was the rational doctor that Mark had known for years. He scratched furiously at his face. "Just some stupid joke, that's all."

*Simon.* The voice was a whisper on the rain, just like the one he thought he heard earlier. Only this time the voice was clear and the tone was demanding. *Simon.*

"Did you hear that?" Mark looked to Jim, who was pale and shaking, trying unsuccessfully to light a cigarette.

"That wasn't real," Jim said, not bothering to look at Mark.

Mark swept past him, ran through the hospital doors, and up the stairs. He rushed past the empty nurse's station and back to Simon's room.

## 4.

When Mark reached the room, Simon was out of bed and standing at the window, looking down into the parking lot as if he were waiting for someone to visit.

"I saw it," Mark said.

"He's an ugly one, huh?" said Simon, continuing to look out the window. "He's not happy I showed you his face. He didn't want too many people to see him like that."

"We have to leave," Mark said. Simon's clothes were not in the room, and all he had was the hospital gown. It didn't matter. Mark would get in the car with his brother and they would drive away from the hospital, away from those damned woods in Silver Point and away from the *thing* on Simon's camera.

"I can't go anywhere he won't come for me." He used the palm of his bandaged hand to scratch his neck. "It's okay though. I'll go with him nice."

"What are you talking about?" Mark said, pulling the blanket from the bed, ready to wrap it around his brother's shoulders so they could flee. Small white things fell from the blanket to the floor where they started wriggling and crawling. Worms, Mark thought in disgust. Worms. Were they from Simon?

As if in answer to the unasked question, Simon turned away from the window to face his brother.

Pockmarks were visible on Simon's soft round face and Mark could see tiny worms poking their heads out of the pus-filled holes. Tears stung Mark's eyes. He choked back the urge to vomit.

"He's coming for me now," Simon said. "I'm already turning to mush on the inside. If I go with him, maybe he'll sleep a bit longer, maybe he won't take you too."

"No. We'll just get out of here." Mark didn't know what else to say. What did you say to someone who had worms easing their way through their skin?

"He says he hasn't eaten since the white meat pushed the red meat out of the woods here. I don't know what that means, but I just know he's hungry. He won't let me go, but maybe I can tell him to let you go."

A part of Mark had the urge to run, to leave Simon alone in the cold hospital and find somewhere safe to hide, a place where he could get away from the night's insanity. He didn't though. He stayed with his brother just as he had done his entire life.

Simon's voice softened. "Maybe you will be able to live now, like you're supposed to live."

Mark looked into Simon's eyes, brown and soft like always. "I can't let you go. You're my brother. We're supposed to be together, no matter what."

Simon smiled. "You always protected me from everything. You saved me from people that would hit me when we were little. You saved me from that crazy squirrel that threw acorns. You gave me a good life, even when Dad and Mom were gone. You loved me."

"I still love you," Mark said, weeping freely. "We gotta go."

"I love you too. If I don't go, he'll eat you. Let me be a big brother and take care of you now."

A shadow spilled into the room as something massive blocked the doorframe. Mark didn't have to turn around (he didn't dare) to know that the God of Worms, the thing from Simon's pictures, stood behind him. The same fetid stench of rotten leaves from the woods now filled the room.

Simon began to walk past Mark, who reached out and grabbed hold of his arm, trying to hold him back. Already worms were beginning to burrow from Simon's arms and chest, to chew their way through the hospital gown. Mark could feel them wiggling on his palms where he held Simon's arm. He didn't care and held tight.

"No!" Simon said.

Simon shoved him easily to the floor. Mark fell hard, felt his head smack the floor and the air whoosh from his lungs. He looked up to see Simon take the hand of the wormy creature in the doorway. Through tears, he watched them walk into the hall. He heard his brother speaking to the creature. "But you promised. That's not fair, not at all."

When the breath finally came back to his lungs, Mark tried to sit up. His head spun. Another sensation quickly came over him though. He realized, with growing revulsion, that his hands burned and itched and that inside it felt as though something was wriggling, growing. He scrambled to his feet and then followed Simon and the God of Worms into the rain, the second in a legion of followers to come.

# LAST MAGIC

The house was full of people singing nonsense carols about snowmen and angels. The tall spruce stood in the living room, decorated with tinsel and bright twinkling lights, the smells of Christmas Eve dinner were thick in the air. All of the children were there with their spouses. The grandchildren were there as well, their laughter punctuating the songs. Yet, the house seemed empty to William and his mind was far from the festivities.

This was the first Christmas he would spend without Karen, the love of his life for more than forty years.

William stood alone in the living room, staring out the picture window. The world outside was a soft shade of blue, white, and gray. The cold colors of winter and of loneliness, he thought. His gaze drifted across the snow-covered field to the trees beyond, and then lifted skyward. Clouds were gathering for a Christmas snow.

As he watched the clouds, he thought of his grandfather. His Grandfather Alden had once said. *The world is never a lonelier place than in the dead of winter, when heavy snow rips limbs from old trees and buries the land in an icy tomb.* William had never felt so lonely in his life.

A sudden tug at his sweater sleeve – the kind of tugging that only a child can produce – tore him from his brooding. He looked down to see Ginny, his four-year-old granddaughter looking up at him with huge brown eyes and a face covered in cookie crumbs.

"Tell me a story, Grandpa Will," she said.

"I'm fresh out, bub," William said, running a hand through her thick, dark hair.

Ginny shook her head. "Impossible."

William smiled. *Impossible* was Ginny's new favorite word, and she had been using it to describe everything since she and her parents arrived that morning. Breakfast had been *impossible*. Zipping her snowsuit was *impossible*. Now his running out of stories was impossible too.

"Mommy says you know stuff about everything,"

"Oh," William said with a knowing smile, "did Mommy send you in here?"

Ginny nodded. "Yup. She said that if I stay in the kitchen I would get stuck under her feet."

William laughed for the first time all day. It was his first laugh in many days actually. "Well, I wouldn't want that to happen."

He eased himself into his favorite chair, an old and battered recliner that Karen had begged him to get rid of for years, and pulled Ginny up onto his lap.

She snuggled into the crook of her grandfather's arm. "You can start now."

The only story in William's head was one that he had been repeating to himself since Karen's death; it was all he had to keep himself going.

"Okay, Ginny, now listen carefully, because this story is true, no matter how *impossible* it may seem."

"M'kay."

William took a deep breath. "A long time ago, when my Grandfather Alden was a boy, he had a dog named Shadow. He loved his dog very much. Shadow followed Grandfather Alden everywhere, even to Sunday school."

"They let a dog in the school!"

"Well, as I understand it, they weren't very happy about it – and don't tell Mommy I told you this – Shadow took a poop in the pews."

Ginny burst out laughing, and then quickly cupped her hand over her mouth. "I wish I had a dog like Shadow," she whispered.

"Yeah, Shadow was a great dog, but one day he got sick. The doggy doctors couldn't fix him. He died and Grandfather Alden was very sad."

"That's not a very good story," Ginny said with downcast eyes.

"It's not over," William said. "You see, Grandfather Alden knew how to bring him back."

"Impossible."

"Nope, it's true," William said.

"How? Like Jesus? Or like a vampire?"

"Neither. Grandfather Alden was from the Old Country, where they still believed in magic."

"Really?"

William nodded. "All kinds of magic. Now, Grandfather Alden knew there was magic in Christmas snow. On Christmas Eve, he used magic to conjure a storm, and then he made a wooden carving of Shadow. That night he trudged out into the forest to find the oldest, most massive oak tree there."

"What's a 'folk tree'?"

"Oak tree, Ginny, *oak*."

"Then what did he do?"

"Well, he cut his finger with a silver knife and dripped blood onto the statue. Then he put the Shadow statue under the tree and waited. The whole time he closed his eyes and thought about how much he loved Shadow. Before long, Shadow came running through the trees, as spry as a puppy."

"Really?"

"That's the story he told me when I was about your age. I believe because it's all I have left to believe. It's the only magic left in me."

She nodded and pursed her lips. "That's nice . . . and sad."

\*\*\*

Ginny stood on tiptoe in front of the picture window, peering out into the gloom. She could barely make out the trees at the field's edge.

"Hey," Ginny's mother said, as she entered the living room. "Didn't you hear me? It's time for bed. Santa Claus will be here soon."

Ginny continued to look out the window. "Grandpa is out there."

"What? Where is he, Gin?"

She spoke with the surety of a tiny sage. "He conquered a storm and went fudging into the woods to find a folk tree and get grandma."

It took a moment for her mother to respond. "Oh, that damn story," she shouted.

Ginny could hear her running through the rest of the house, looking for Grandpa William and waking the others. A few minutes later the sleepy adults were pulling on boots and coats, readying themselves to go outside and look for Grandpa William.

Ginny stayed at the window and watched the snow begin to fall, thick and beautiful.

Her mother and father, along with her aunts and uncles, returned a short time later. They were all crying and saying that they had found him frozen beneath a tree. They tried to whisper, but Ginny could hear them.

Ginny didn't cry though. She was still on tiptoe, staring into the night. Finally, she saw what she had been waiting for. There in the blackness were two translucent figures moving slowly through the trees. They looked as though they were holding hands and Ginny imagined they were smiling and laughing, just like Grandma and Grandpa always did when she came to visit.

Now Ginny could feel herself beginning to cry, but she was smiling at the same time. Grandpa's magic, just like he had told her, was possible.

# ORNAMENTS

"Wicked things crawl around down there," whispered the scraggly haired, dark skinned woman. She pointed a crooked finger at the ancient junkyard secretly nestled in a nameless Southern California valley. She adjusted the dark sunglasses she wore, sucked in a deep breath through cracked lips and her few remaining brown teeth.

Paul took a final drag off his cigarette, let it fall to the ground and then extinguished it with the heel of his boot. He blew the smoke into the cloudless sky and then chuckled at the old woman, flashing his million-dollar smile. "You're name is Blue, isn't it? I was warned about you."

The woman leaned against her shopping cart full of cans, bottles, and ratty blankets. "Who told you 'bout me?"

"Guran, the guy that hired me to get the ornament, said that you would try to stop me from going into the junkyard," he said. Guran had also told him that Blue was bat-shit crazy, but he didn't feel the need to let her know that.

"Well then," the old woman said, seemingly taken aback that Paul knew her name. "You and Guran don't know everything. I wasn't going to tell you not to go down into the junkyard. I just wanted to tell you that

42

strange things end up in that place, all kinds of things you wouldn't like. They don't come out without a price, something that don't nobody want to pay."

Paul smiled at her again. Guran was right about this one – bat-shit crazy, fucking guano loco. Blue scowled at his smile as though she could read his thoughts.

He turned his back to her, gave her a dismissive wave, and started walking down the dirt trail that led down to the junkyard.

The hot sun of the late California afternoon beat down on him as he traipsed down the winding path, kicking up small clouds of dust with every step. He hated to admit it, but Blue had managed to get beneath his skin. The chick was definitely creepy. Still, that wouldn't stop him from his mission.

The job, a surprise offer that came during a binge of alcohol and cocaine, was too good to pass up though. Guran was a wiry old man with wild hair and equally wild eyes, and he always wore eyeglasses that were missing the lenses. Paul had done odd jobs for the man in the past, and even though Guran was eccentric, he was loaded and he paid well. Paul knew enough never to turn down easy money.

This particular job, which Paul knew was probably the easiest job he'd ever had, was simply to retrieve a hood ornament from a 1949 Gargoyle that was supposed to be tucked away somewhere in the junkyard.

The Gargoyle was one of only twenty-four cars of its type in existence, and the hood ornament was supposed to be worth a fortune. Each of the ornaments, little gargoyle statues, was unique. Collectors would pay ungodly sums for them; at least that's what Guran had told him.

Currently, Guran owned four of the ornaments. This would be his fifth as long as Paul was able to find it. And when he found it, Guran promised him twenty grand. Paul knew many decadent ways he could blow twenty grand.

According to Guran, the Gargoyle would "lie beneath the Ram." He had told Paul that was what the stars above whispered to him. Paul was not entirely sure what in the hell that meant, and he didn't know how it was going to help him find the thing either. But Paul would crawl across molten rock for as much scratch as Guran was offering, so spending some time in a junk heap was no biggie.

When he reached the edge of the junkyard, the sun was already starting to dip toward the Pacific and cast long shadows across the valley floor. He mentally cursed Blue for wasting his time. He'd planned to get in and out of the junkyard with the gargoyle before darkness fell. Now it looked like he might be scrounging around in the dark. With his luck, he would grab hold of a rattlesnake.

He thought about lighting another cigarette, but the grasses were dead and dry this time of year. The last thing he wanted to do was to start a wildfire. He could smoke all the cigarettes he wanted when he got home. He sighed, tried to push away the desire for nicotine, and then entered the junkyard.

The junkyard was not what he had expected. This place was orderly chaos, if there were such a thing. There were rusting hulks of old cars and trucks stacked neatly atop one another; there were piles of discarded refrigerators and washing machines, towers of eggshell white. Yet, each item seemed to have its specific place as though it were all a giant puzzle. Manicured paths wound neatly between the piles of refuse. With its little streets as they were, the junkyard reminded Paul of a city in miniature. Finding the ornament was going to be a bitch.

An hour later the sun had just about vanished. Night came on fast and brought with it a chill that settled over Paul's sweat-drenched body. He'd searched through several towers of old cars, but hadn't found the gargoyle. The more he explored the junkyard, the stranger it became. It was far larger than he had envisioned, and the paths never seemed to lead to the same place twice. The junkyard seemed to have a mind of its own. He knew it was his imagination, of course, but that didn't stop the nagging in his brain that maybe Blue was right.

Paul dusted his hands on his pants, wiped the sweat from his head with his forearm and caught a glint of metal in the dying sunlight. And there was the ornament, lying atop a rusted hood and beneath the hulk of an old Dodge Ram.

"Are you kidding me," he said, shaking his head. He knew he had just passed this tower of rust and rubber not five minutes before and there was no ornament. Blue's words echoed in his head, *wicked things crawl around down there*. Paul grabbed the gargoyle and felt a shiver run from his tailbone to the nape of his neck.

From the bottom of its scaled feet to the top of its wedge-shaped head, the gargoyle was six inches of pure gaudiness. Its muscular arms ended in sickle shaped claws. Paul couldn't fathom why anyone would want to collect the ugly little things. What did he know? As the saying goes, one man's trash is another man's treasure. After all, he was just an overpaid gopher, with the emphasis on overpaid.

With the ornament in hand and a renewed sense of vigor, he began walking back through the junkyard paths toward the exit.

"Nothing is free." The words, uttered by some unseen entity, seemed to float over the graveyard of junk. For a moment, he wasn't sure that he had heard the words at all, thought that maybe he'd imagined them. Then the voice spoke again. "Something of you goes to the Junkman."

Paul froze, turned his head slowly to look over his shoulder. There! Something moved just outside the range of his vision. The gathering night made it hard to see what it was though.

He began to mutter. "I . . . I didn't know there was a caretaker or anything. I'm sorry for trespassing. I'm going to go now."

"Something of you goes to the Junkman."

Paul wanted to run, to get the hell of the valley and back to a nice bottle of Jack Daniels. He wasn't sure where the voice was coming from though, didn't know which way to turn. He dug into his pants pocket and pulled out a wrinkled ten-dollar bill. "Ten bucks; it's yours."

"Something of *you* goes to the Junkman."

The voice now seemed louder to Paul, and it seemed to be coming from inside his own head. Somewhere else in the junkyard, he could hear the sound of metal scraping against metal.

Screw this. He took off running, not knowing where he was going, and soon found himself lost in the rusted hedge maze. Twists, turns, junctions that he didn't remember from before cropped up and turned him completely around. He had no idea where he was and the sound of the grating metal continued. It seemed to grow louder with each passing second.

Paul finally stopped to catch his breath. He held tight to the gargoyle, its metal digging into the palm of his sweat-slicked hand. He looked down at the thing and thought of tossing it away. No. only an idiot throws twenty grand.

A hand grasped his shoulder, gripping like iron, spinning him around. The Junkman, he thought, staring into the face of the thing that held him tight. What he saw could not really be a face though.

The Junkman, the *thing*, had no hair, no nose, and no mouth – just a pair of deep brown eyes and one small ear that looked like it belonged to an infant set on a fleshy, pale head. The rest of the thing's body was an amalgam of refuse, metal, and flesh. In its hollow stomach were rotted leaves and pieces of a mutilated cat. One of its legs was thick, corded muscle and sinew while the other was made of metal pipes and dark fur. Its arms were twisted metal, somehow fused together to allow fluid movement. Its fingers ended in knives and straight razors.

Paul struggled, the grip tightened. He began to hammer the thing's head with the gargoyle in his hand, opening a long gash along its face. The blood that oozed from the gash stank like wet garbage. Paul gagged and the grip grew tighter still.

"Something of you goes to the Junkman."

\*\*\*

"I warned him."

Paul knew that voice . . . the old woman, Blue.

47

He could hear her clearly. Slowly, painfully, he opened his eyes and stared up into her wrinkled face. Beyond her, he could see the bright blue sky. Where was he? How long had he been there? What happened?

"Poor stupid thing," she said, helping him to sit up. "He don't even realize it yet."

He felt the ornament still in his hand, digging into his flesh. He held it up and another figure suddenly popped into his line of sight. Guran.

"You did wonderful work, boy," Guran said, leering at the gargoyle.

Paul tried to open his mouth, to tell Guran to *fuck off,* but he couldn't. He couldn't open his mouth at all.

*Something of you goes to the Junkman.*

"He gets it now," Blue said, taking off her sunglasses. Where her eyes should have been were only flaps of skin sunk into the ocular orbits of her skull.

Paul's own eyes widened and he reached up to touch his mouth, finding only smooth flesh. He tried in vain to scream.

# THE DEAD DON'T

Hannah sat with her back against a large oak, her mind teetering at insanity's jagged edge. The night air pressed against her naked flesh, but she was not cold. How wonderful would it be, she wondered, to fall into that abyss, a place where it did not matter if the world made any sense?

At her feet was a long and shallow hole, newly dug. It confused her. She did not know where she was, and she knew very little of whom she was. She had a name. Hannah. Other names came to her. Jerry. Jacob. They were just names.

She found that her limbs were stiff when she tried to move. Slowly, she brought fingers to her chest and touched the still fresh Y-shaped wound that ran from her chest to her navel. A thought came to her. It could not be an autopsy incision, because . . . .

She began to probe the wound, to pull apart the poor stitching and dip her fingers into the gaping cavity beneath. A dull throb rocked her body.

Inside she was empty, completely hollowed out.

No. No, that cannot be. The Dead *don't* think. The Dead *don't* walk.

She reached deeper until her fingers grazed her spine. With no lungs, she could not even scream; she let her mind do it for her.

A distant light through the forest caught her attention. She stood on stiff legs and began to walk toward it, unsure of what it was and hoping that the source of the light might provide answers. Branches snagged at her hair, briars ripped her dead flesh, as though the forest was trying to stop her. Hannah continued.

Images, like poor quality snapshots, began to flash in her head. Smiling parents, friends and lovers she could not quite recall, all flickered in her mind. Her wedding, her husband Jacob, their son Jerry, all of them flashed before her. Sweet little Jerry, so tiny. Thoughts of the baby warmed her hollow insides.

She came closer to the light and the memory of the crash slammed into her. The winding backwoods roads that led to her in-law's place in Silver Point, the large rock that shattered the windshield, her screams mingled with the baby's cries as the car veered off the road; the memories kept coming. The man dressed in dark clothing that came to pull them free of the car before blackness engulfed her. Yes, she remembered him now.

The source of light was coming from a small shack. Hannah could hear movements and sounds coming from within. A child's cry; her child's cry.

Hannah shambled to the hovel and climbed the weathered steps to the porch. She made her way to the window, where she could see through the ragged curtains into the shack.

Hanging from chains on the ceiling were the skinned carcasses of many small animals. A rusty color stained the floor from where their life dripped during skinning. On a small wooden table, she could see a heart, lungs, and other organs, all of which were too large to be anything but her own.

A tall, slender man at the rear of the shack was stirring a large kettle that sat atop a wood-burning stove. Nine-month-old Jerry hung naked and upside down from the ceiling, shrieking and wiggling. His powder blue blanket lay neatly folded on the floor.

Rage filled the hollow where her organs once lived. She began to pound on the shack's thin walls.

The lanky cook turned around, wooden spoon in his hand. His face was not the monster Hannah had expected. He was clean-shaven and his hair was neatly trimmed, but his eyes were predatory. He wiped a hand on the leather apron he wore and licked his lips.

He dropped the spoon into the kettle and picked up a hatchet from an array of bladed tools near the stove.

Hannah watched as he made his way across the blood-caked floor, wanting him to come to her.

"Who's there?" His voice was small, almost feminine.

Hannah pounded harder on the walls, wanting to get to him, wanting to jab her fingers into his eyes and shut them forever.

"Shit," he said. "Shit, shit, shit." He started toward the door, hatchet raised.

Jerry cried harder, sending Hannah into a deeper rage. When the man opened the door, Hannah was there. She lunged at him, teeth bared. He opened his mouth to scream, but she latched onto his throat with one of her hands and squeezed. His mouth worked like a gasping fish, and he buried the hatchet into her clavicle.

Hannah hardly noticed.

She took him to the floor, crushing and twisting his windpipe. His eyes turned from those of a predator to frightened prey. With her dirt-encrusted nails, she tore out huge gobs of his flesh, leaving him to twitch and die on the dirty floor.

***

Jerry was still crying when she took him down from the chains. She cradled him in her cold arms and rocked him until he fell asleep.

Though she could not feel it, she was sure the night was cold even inside the shack. She could not stay there any longer. The un-life that she had been given – by either vengeful angels or laughing demons – was starting to fade.

She wrapped Jerry in his blanket, tucked him inside her torso to keep him from the wind and the cold, and headed down the dirt driveway from the shack to the road. A car would pass soon enough. She could rest and Jerry could go home.

Jason M. Tucker

# BALLAD OF THE PALE RIDERS

*They ride into the Outlands whenever there's a need*
*Push on through the darkness on the backs o' their brave steeds*
*They blaze a trail across the twisted land of living dead*
*Steadying their rifles as they aim for the heads*
*Aim for the heads...aim for the heads...aim for the heads*

---excerpt from the folk tune
*Ballad of the Pale Riders*

## 1.

Thomas Johns looked over his shoulder at the worn trail that twisted through the field and over an old strand of highway behind him. He squinted, thinking he saw something moving in the late afternoon gloom.

The asphalt along the highway had cracked long ago and weeds broke through in a number of places, waving at him in the wind, and he was sure that must have been what caught his attention. Like so many areas in the Outlands, nature was reasserting its dominance.

"Nothing back there," said Gareth, his voice gruff as usual. "You keep looking over your shoulder like that and a Rot or an Eater will hit you from the front. Keep your eyes forward; use the rest of your senses to scan the environment. Watch your horse and the way she acts. She'll tell you plenty if you only pay attention. If you can't learn to do that, you'll end up dead real quick."

Thomas snapped his head forward and looked up the trail at the back of Gareth Pope sitting astride a large white horse, a black, wide brimmed cowboy hat pulled tight onto his head. That was the most the man had said to him the past two days they'd been together.

"Sorry," Thomas said. Gareth grunted and mumbled something that Thomas couldn't make out.

He stared at the back of Gareth's thin form. Black hair peppered with gray leaked out from beneath the hat.

Gareth was legendary, a Pale Rider who had traveled the Outlands, fought cannibals and the undead for more than four decades. He was one of the original thirteen Pale Riders. Of that original bunch, he was the only one still living and riding. Legend even told that Gareth saw and fought in the fall of Chicago along with Granger Black, but Thomas hadn't had the nerve to bring it up in the week he'd known the man.

Even though he was now nearing his mid fifties, the Rider showed no signs of slowing, and he seemed to have the vigor of a man half his age.

Gareth was a different breed and he frightened Thomas. Thomas was unused to people like the Rider, people who spat and cursed, smoked and drank shine out of backroom stills. He had lived in luxury with his parents until he volunteered in the Wall Militia, where he was an officer. His assignment to the Pale Riders had come as a surprise.

Well, not exactly as a surprise. He knew there would be some sort of repercussion for spending so much time between the legs of the Division Chief's daughter. Still, he never imagined it would lead him to join the ranks of the Pale Riders. That was as good as a death sentence.

The Pale Riders were the only ones who braved deep into the Outlands. They rode alone or in small groups carrying messages or ferrying travelers from one walled city to the next. It was a suicide job. Packs of the undead Rots hunted the wild lands, and so did the Eaters, groups of savage cannibals. The only safe havens outside of the walled cities were the stick villages, which were little more than frontier towns that were, as the name suggested, out in the sticks. They were full of outlaws too. Dirty little places like that, Gareth thought, must be just as bad as the Outlands themselves.

All he had to do was stay alive long enough to have his parents to square things away with the Division Chief. Nothing a few political favors couldn't cure.

"Are we nearing the next campsite," Thomas asked. His body ached from being on the horse; he wasn't used to it.

"We aren't staying at one of the sites tonight. We're riding through to Whitehall," Gareth said.

"That's a stick town," Thomas said, not bothering to hide his displeasure. His horse whinnied and shook her head, but Thomas paid little attention. "That's miles out of the way. I don't think we need to stop there. Don't you have a package to deliver?"

Gareth continued to keep his eyes forward, but his voice was clipped and cold. "Don't give a shit what you think, and the package will get there when it gets there. I tell you what to do and where to go. If you want to live, all you need to do is to listen.

"If a Rider sticks to the same exact trail every time he comes out of a Wall, then the Eaters and the Rots are going to figure that out real quick. You change what you do; you don't make patterns. You thick or you got it?"

Thomas's face was flush. No one had spoken to him like that when he was an officer. And now this filthy Rider was spouting off to him as if he were a child.

"While you're sitting there on top of your horse, getting all pissed off at me, you should be looking to the northwest, twenty yards out," Gareth said. "Take care of it."

It took Thomas a moment to register what Gareth had just said, but he turned his head to the left and saw it lumbering toward them.

The bear had been dead for God knew how long. The plague that brought the dead back to life had a way of slowing decay. The beast's stomach, torn partially open, had dried intestines spilling though. Patches of fur and skin were missing, as was one of the bear's eyes. Its mouth and teeth appeared to be in good working order though.

Thomas had never seen an undead animal before. Sights such as that weren't part of city life, and he'd never had the stomach to watch any of the snuff films starring undead humans and animals, that would sometimes play in illegal theaters in rough parts of the city.

He fumbled with his rifle, which was an ancient Winchester lever action, nothing like the automatics he trained with as part of the Wall Militia. The damned Pale Riders prided themselves on using old weapons straight out of the Wild West: rifles, revolvers, and only the biggest knives. The knife he wore on his belt now still seemed foreign to him, useless.

Thomas brought the rifle to his shoulder and aimed. He was surprised to see just how much distance the bear had made in those seconds it took to take aim. It was only about thirty feet away.

He fired and a bullet tore through the bear's shoulder. It didn't notice the wound and kept coming. Beneath him, his horse began to shake. He knew she was a warhorse, trained not to run but to fight the undead by slamming hooves through their skulls. Still, the bear seemed to unnerve her. He aimed again but couldn't get a steady shot; the bullet went high and the bear came closer.

Another shot rang out, and Thomas saw the skull and brains of the beast explode out of the right side of its head. It fell without a twitch.

Thomas turned and saw Gareth lower his own rifle. "Is that what they teach you in the Militia?"

"I… I'm not used to this rifle. We had automatics."

"Automatics jam. How many undead have you killed anyway?"

"Enough," Thomas said, lying. Officers told grunts to kill undead. They didn't do it themselves. Truth was that Thomas had never killed anything in his life, which was a damn difficult feat in a world overrun with zombies and savages. But he was privileged and proud of it. Others could to the killing. Until now, that was.

Gareth looked at Thomas for a moment. Thomas thought he saw the man's features soften briefly, but they stiffened quickly.

"You know," said Gareth, "they sent you out here to die. They figure if the Outlands don't get you then you might just be depressed enough to put a bullet in your own brain. Either way you'd be dead."

Thomas nodded, reloaded his rifle and placed it into the makeshift holster alongside his saddle.

"But," Gareth continued, "I don't like the folks that run the Walls very much, so I ain't about to let the Outlands get you. I'll train you and I'll keep you alive as long as you don't piss me off too much. If you do then I might just kill you myself."

As Gareth turned his horse around and headed down the trial once more, Thomas thought he saw a slight smile play across the Rider's features.

## 2.

Darkness had just settled across the land and the full moon was beginning its ride high into the sky when Thomas saw Whitehall in the distance.

The stick village had a makeshift wall made from timber, junked vehicles that were useless since fuel ran out, and just about anything else people could find to shore up the walls. They were nothing like the thick concrete walls around the cities of New Boston and Albany, where Thomas grew up. These walls didn't look sturdy, not at all.

He followed Gareth up to the gates, which were made of wood and what looked like metal siding.

Gareth called out and there was sudden movement on the top of the wall. A tiny, thin man with a wiry beard and thick eyebrows poked his head over the top. When he saw Gareth, his face split into a wide and toothless grin.

"Well," the figure called down to them, "if it ain't a Pale Rider in the flesh. You ain't been out this way in a spell."

"I'm here now," said Gareth.

"What you got with you down there?" the man said, gesturing with his head toward Thomas.

"Fodder," said Gareth. "Now, Roman, how 'bout you let us inside before something decides to come up and gnaw on us."

Roman disappeared from the top of the wall. Before long, Thomas heard a grinding sound. The gate slowly rose until there was room for the men and their horses to enter. As soon as they were through, the portcullis slammed shut.

"Hey," Roman called. He stood on a walkway that ran the length of the wall. Thomas could see two other men on the wall, their eyes trained into the Outlands as though they were anticipating something.

Gareth turned to look up at Roman.

"You bring me anything good? Skin mags, a bottle of professional hooch?" the old man asked.

"Not this time. Maybe on our way back through," Gareth said. Then he asked, "Paula in a good mood lately?"

Roman laughed. "Paula ain't ever in a good mood."

"I notice you got some extra eyes up there with you this evening. Trouble?" Gareth nodded toward the men who still kept watch.

"Had some of those damn cannibals sniffing around here the past couple days. I think they was trying to find a way in or something," Roman said, shrugging. He looked over his shoulder into the gloom of the Outlands. "Filthy damn Eaters. They're as bad as the Rots."

"How many of the undead have you seen lately?" asked Thomas.

"So the fodder speaks," said Roman, turning his attention toward Thomas. "Haven't seen any in a month at least. Maybe they're finally thinning out."

"No, they won't thin out until everything's dead," said Gareth. "I hear from some of the other Riders that the San Diego Wall fell about a month or two ago. Thousands of the damn Rots just poured into the city from down south. Came right out of the water too. We ain't seen that before."

Roman bowed his head. "Damn…San Diego, huh?"

Thomas felt his throat tighten. He hadn't heard anything about a Wall City ever being overrun. Things like that just didn't happen. If it did, then everything he learned and everything people believed about being safe in the cities was a lie. If San Diego could fall, so could Albany or New Boston. Why wouldn't they tell the people?

"Keep your eyes sharp." Gareth nodded at Roman and then urged his horse forward, heading deeper into the stick town. Thomas followed reluctantly, still thinking about San Diego.

The few roads in Whitehall were all made of dirt, and they all connected to Main Street, which held the handful of businesses the town boasted. Some children had gathered along the street and were watching, waving, and whispering as Gareth rode past. They seemed to regard the Rider with awe.

As Thomas looked at the buildings, he realized he could barely call them businesses at all. There was a general store, a bar, and a small medical center that looked like it had never seen good days. On side streets were a number of ramshackle houses and beyond that the farms and livestock pens. Beyond them the encompassing wall. The place stank of animals and sweat. To Thomas, it was Hell.

They stopped at the unnamed bar and handed the reins of their horses over to a young boy with a dirty face who took the animals around the back to bathe them, feed them, and settle them for the evening. Thomas followed Gareth up the creaky wooden steps and through the front door.

Lantern light and candles illuminated the bar's interior and showed that it was as dilapidated as the rest of the town, though it did have a fireplace with several comfortable looking chairs and a tattered sofa placed in front of it. The bar was empty save for an attractive woman who stood behind the bar counter. Her skin was dark and her short-cropped hair had bits of gray sprinkled throughout. She looked up when Gareth and Thomas entered, and grimaced.

"Well, Mr. Pope," she said to Gareth, "I didn't know if you were ever coming back this way. Thought maybe you had finally got yourself eaten."

"'Hell, I'm too bitter for the cannibals and too smart for the Rots. By the way, it's good to see you too, Paula," he said, taking off his hat and setting it on the bar. She placed two dirty shot glasses on the bar and filled them with a thick yellow liquid that smelled like alcohol, honey, and rotten milk. Gareth pushed one of the shot glasses toward Thomas.

"Thanks," Thomas said, looking at the glass. He wasn't much of a drinker, and he had no idea what the thick liquid was. He sniffed it, then set the glass down again and then eased himself onto a barstool. Then he groaned as he realized just how much his ass hurt from riding on that damned horse the past two days.

"So, Roman tells me that some Eaters have been bothering the walls, trying to find a way inside," said Gareth.

"Yeah," Paula said, "I swear they're worse than the Rots."

"You mean the savages are so desperate for food that they'll take to trying to break into a fortified town?" Thomas was horrified. He'd heard stories of the Eaters kidnapping people in the dead of night and bringing them back to their caves and into deep hollows where they would roast them alive. He hadn't believed it, yet the Outlands were proving to be a true nightmare.

"They're coming for more than food. They want to take people to mate. Happens every couple of years," said Paula, shuddering. "That's how they keep their gangs going."

"That's terrible," Thomas said, feeling sudden pity for the people that lived in the dirty little town. At the same time, he felt frustrated with them. Why wouldn't they just move into one of the walled cities?

"Whitehall got enough people on the wall?" Gareth asked. "Eaters are savage, but they aren't stupid."

"Wall ain't my job. I get people drunk enough to think it ain't as bad as it is. And I wait for you to ride though every few months." Thomas watched as Paula's hand lingered on Gareth's for just a moment. He turned his eyes away before Gareth could catch him staring.

"Tell you what," Paula said, "I'll get you and your little friend something to eat," Paula said, turning away and heading through a door behind the bar.

Gareth grabbed his shot, tilted his head back and upended the glass to let the yellow liquid slide into his mouth. He swallowed and then turned to Thomas. "Drink up. It'll keep you warm, make you think straight."

"I don't drink much," Thomas said. "What is it anyway?"

"They call it Mash. It keeps you going. Come on, drink up like a man," said Gareth, looking at Thomas from the corner of his eyes. "It tastes better than it smells by the way."

Thomas reached for the glass and slurped down the Mash. At once, his throat felt as though it was on fire and then the sickly sweet taste hit him, reminding him slightly of vomit.

Gareth laughed and patted him on the back. "Actually, it tastes just like it smells."

The taste lingered on his tongue, but a flood of warmth and peace suddenly overcame him.

"Good shit, right?" said Gareth, reaching behind the bar and grabbing a bottle. "One more each; don't tell Paula."

"Did they really breach San Diego's wall? Is it gone?" The question had been weighing on his mind since he heard Gareth tell the man at the gate. Now, he figured, when Gareth was in a talking mood, was the best time to ask.

Gareth nodded. "It fell. It's gone, but I'm sure some folk got out. Sad thing is they don't know how to live in the Outlands. They won't last long."

"Other Riders told you?"

"Yup," said Gareth, pouring more of the Mash into his and Thomas's glass.

"Why hasn't anyone in Albany been told?"

"The politicians know. They choose not to tell folks." Gareth said.

"Because they don't want people to worry," said Thomas.

"Not exactly." Gareth swallowed his second shot of Mash. "It's because they want to remain in control. It is hard to control a people that are panicked. They like the power they got and they don't wanna change, won't change until something comes up and bites them on the ass."

Bullshit, Thomas thought.

"That's why stick villages exist," Gareth continued. "Folks out here might be a bit dirtier, and they might not have all the luxuries of people holed up inside places like Albany, but they don't have to deal with lying politicians and being told what to do and where to work. People out here got it rough, but they're free."

The warm feeling in his stomach remained, but the sense of peace was gone. Instead, Thomas felt numb, and he barely noticed as Paula returned to the room with two plates of small potatoes.

"This is what I got," she said, placing the plates in front of them. "I know it's better than the dried stuff you eat."

The two began eating, shoveling the potatoes into their mouths until the plates were clean. Then Paula asked, "What are you delivering this time? A package or your sidekick here?"

Gareth patted his pocket and said, "Package."

Paula turned her attention toward Thomas now. "Why are you riding with Gareth? You look too clean to be associated with the likes of him."

Gareth laughed. "He is clean. Thomas Johns here was a shiny officer in Albany before he got messed up with me. He's training to become a Rider."

"You must've pissed somebody off real good, huh?" Paula said.

"Something like that," said Thomas, suddenly realizing how exhausted he was. It must be the Mash, he thought.

Gareth and Paula talked for a few more minutes, but Thomas couldn't make out what they were saying. Flirting, he thought, but all Thomas could think about was sleep.

He remembered stumbling toward the couch near the fireplace and seeing Gareth and Paula, hand in hand, retreating to another room. Then he closed his eyes and let the Mash induced sleep overtake him.

## 3.

Thomas awoke to what sounded like a distant cry for help. He opened his eyes and stared up into the darkness, wondering if he'd actually heard anything. He lay still for a moment and listened. Another scream, this one louder, closer, and more insistent; it was no mere leftover from a nightmare.

A second later, he heard movement from the other room. Gareth came into the bar followed by Paula, who was holding a lantern.

"Up," said Gareth, kicking the couch as he passed.

"I am" said Thomas, standing up. "What's the problem?"

"How am I supposed to know? I just woke up," Gareth said, shaking his head at Thomas.

Someone suddenly began pounding on the bar's front door. Gareth's revolver was in his hand and aimed at the door before Thomas even had time to register the knock.

"Who's there?" shouted Paula.

Thomas could see that she was holding a handgun as well, an automatic. She leveled it at the door. He withdrew his own revolver and found that his hands were shaking, moist with cool sweat. More screams resounded from outside.

"It's Roman," the voice on the other side hollered. Thomas recognized the voice of the old man from the wall.

Paula ran to the door, unlocked and opened it, and Roman fell through. In the lantern light, Thomas could see that the old man was bleeding from a gash on the side of his head. He and Gareth both hurried over to the doorway.

"What happened?" Thomas knelt at Roman's side and inspected the wound. He had some basic first aid training, but he couldn't see how deep the wound was. He knew that even surface wounds on the head would bleed profusely, and there was no way he could tell just how serious it was in the low light.

"Eaters," Gareth yelled. "They're taking off!"

Roman reached up, grabbed Thomas's shirt collar and pulled downward. The old man's eyes were wild and his breath smelled sour. It was hot on Thomas's face when Roman said, "Pulled down part of the wall and came through . . . grabbing the little ones, the girls."

Then it was true, Thomas thought. The Eaters came for mates as well as meat.

Gareth smacked Thomas on the shoulder. "Let's go. You go 'round back and get our horses; Paula can take care of Roman."

"Where are you going," Thomas said. It would be pure suicide for Gareth to ride out against the Eaters, and he had to deliver his package after all. Getting information to the other walled cities was the duty of the Pale Rider, and that was more important than some stick village.

"I'm going to get those kids back."

"Like hell you are," said Thomas, surprising himself. He thought it must have been something instilled from his training as an officer. "You have a delivery to make. Don't they have lawmen that can handle this?"

The next thing Thomas knew, Gareth's leathery hand was wrapped around his throat and squeezing. Gareth shook Thomas by the neck, smashing the back of his head into the doorframe. The impact sent bright stars dancing before Thomas's eyes.

"Pale Riders are the law out here, and I plan on helping those kids," Gareth whispered. "I'm losing time because of you. Now saddle up our horses or else I'll skin you when I get back."

When Gareth let go of his throat, Thomas found himself shaking. He didn't know if it was from rage or fear. He looked at Gareth, who was already helping Paula take Roman to the couch.

Thomas, still not used to taking orders, sped to the stables at the back of the bar to ready the horses.

## 4.

The Eaters' trail was easy to follow. The savages were on foot – Eater's weren't only cannibals, but they were also connoisseurs of horseflesh and would rather eat the beasts than ride them – and they didn't bother to cover up their tracks. Even Thomas could see where they were going by the light of the full moon.

Gareth pushed his stallion hard, and it was all Thomas's mare could do to keep up with the other horse. The Eaters and their captives were in sight within fifteen minutes of leaving Whitehall. Thomas could see the silhouettes of a number of figures hurrying across an old two-lane road and into a wide grassy area. Beyond the field were the remnants of a small town, something that existed before the plague.

Gareth's horse slowed. He raised his fist, which Thomas recognized as a signal to stop. He slowed his mare and came up alongside Gareth.

"Is that were they live?" Thomas asked. His throat still hurt from where Gareth has nearly squeezed the life out of him less than half an hour before.

"No," said Gareth. "They wouldn't live this close to Whitehall. They're stopping there to take inventory of their catch, maybe even test out the merchandise. I doubt they have any idea they've even been followed."

"You've seen this kind of thing before?"

"Out here, you get to see all kinds of shit. This is just one of a million different fucked up things that go on."

Thomas looked from Gareth to the dark townscape half a mile across the field. Most of the buildings were rubble, torn apart years ago when the undead first rose.

Jason M. Tucker

The only structure that looked like it was intact was a church. Thomas could see the steeple rising like a spear in the darkness.

"How do you not go insane, knowing things like this happen?"

"No one ever accused me of being sane," Gareth said. "If I was, do you think I'd be doing this? Do you think I'd be a Rider? Kid, you do what you can make things a little better for the people out here. They don't have anybody but us Riders. You'll learn that, I hope. That's one of the few things that'll keep you going when the rest of the world is nothing but shit."

Thomas digested what Gareth said, remembering the faces of the children as they watched the Rider. He remembered the songs about the Riders that his nanny sang to him as a child. The Riders were helping to tame a wicked land, but the officer inside of him still cringed at the thought of shirking duty. He hated many things about Gareth, and he really didn't understand the man. However, he respected him despite his insolence.

The sound of crying drifted across the open field.

"What's the plan?"

"Kill the Eaters," said Gareth, spurring his horse forward. "And try to aim better than you did at that bear earlier, huh? I don't feel like getting shot by the likes of you."

Thomas tried to smile, but found that he was shaking too much to start even a semblance of a grin. He dug his own spurs into the mare and she broke into a run, following Gareth's horse closely.

The horses thundered across the field and before Thomas knew it, they were nearing the edge of the broken town. Gareth yelled something but Thomas couldn't hear over the sound of hooves.

Thomas knew then that something was wrong. It was a trap. His mare's head twitched, almost imperceptibly toward the left and he followed with his eyes. One of the Eaters, a man wearing ragged clothing and with a face painted black with charcoal. The savage hid in the crumbled foundation of a house. The Eater's arm suddenly cocked back, ready to throw what looked to Thomas like a large rock.

Thomas ducked as the rock sailed over his head. He slowed the mare and slid off while simultaneously pulling the rifle from the sheath near his saddle. Using the saddle to steady his shot, he aimed at the Eater who had thrown the rock and squeezed the trigger. The bullet smashed into the Eater's chest and he dropped to the ground, dead. The clean shot surprised Thomas.

"Better," Gareth said. "Let's go."

"Where are the others?"

"My bet is that church. That fellow," he said, gesturing toward the dead Eater, "was their lookout. We have to finish this business quick. The sound of gunfire draws the Rots out of the woodwork. Every undead critter in a mile will be swarming this place. I don't feel much like having to fight with them tonight too."

Thomas wondered just how many of the undead could still be wandering the woods, hidden and waiting. Images of dead animals and people filled his head and he did his best to shake them from his mind's eye. He had other things to worry about now.

"Let's get it over with," Thomas said.

"Quick as a rabbit," Gareth said. "The other Eaters must have heard the gunshots, so they'll be expecting us."

"How many of them are there?"

"Six left by my count now that that fellow is dead," Gareth said. "They have five captives."

They left the horses at the edge of town. The beasts were trained to stay and wait for the Riders, but they were intelligent enough to run should the need arise.

The moment that Gareth and Thomas started toward the church, they saw three dark forms racing down the street toward them, half-crouched and carrying straight blades that glinted in the light of the moon.

"Just like that they're coming at us?" Thomas asked.

"That's only three of them," said Gareth.

"What about the others?"

"Remember earlier when I told you not to look behind you?"

"Yes."

"Well, now's your chance to have a look back there since I know how much you enjoy it," Gareth said. His rifle was already at his shoulder. He fired and dropped one of the advancing Eaters.

Thomas spun around and could see the remaining two Eaters creeping through the shadows. He raised his rifle, aimed, and held his breath to steady himself just before taking the shot. It caught the nearest Eater in the stomach, sent him screaming to the ground. The second Eater ducked into the shadows.

Another shot from Gareth and a shout of surprise from an Eater told Thomas that the Rider's second shot had hit its mark.

Thomas was trying to find his second target that had vanished into the gloom. A flash of moonlight on metal off to his left caught his attention and then the

Eater was upon him, knocking the rifle from his hands and forcing him to the ground.

The Eater, face blackened with charcoal like the others, wore a necklace made of finger bones that dangled in Thomas's face. He tried to push the Eater, but the savage was wiry and strong.

Thomas tried to call for Gareth, but the Eater clamped a hand across his mouth before he could get the words out. Thomas bit down onto the Eater's hand, but the savage just smiled and raised a long straight knife in his other hand and readied a strike.

With a surge of strength, Thomas used one hand to push the Eater upwards a few inches until he could grab his own knife from his belt. Thomas jammed his knife into the Eater's gut, impaling him. The Eater continued to smile as he died.

Thomas quickly rolled the Eater off him and pulled himself to his feet just in time to see Gareth smash the butt of his rifle into another Eater's blackened face, dropping him to the ground. As soon as the Eater fell, Gareth unsheathed his Bowie and slit the Eater's throat.

Thomas pulled his own knife from the body of the man he had just killed and wiped the blood on the rags in which the Eater was dressed.

"There's one missing," Thomas said.

"It'll be at the church making sure the kids don't run off," Gareth said, as he reloaded his rifle. "Come on."

They hurried across to the doors of the church, and they could hear the kids crying inside. Gareth kicked the door open and rushed inside with Thomas following right after.

The inside of the church was unlit save for shafts of pale moonlight that filtered in through the holes in the roof. The pews were long gone, the floor vast and empty except for the children huddled in the corner where the last Eater stood guard over them.

Gareth didn't waste time. In mid stride, he shot the Eater in the center of the skull and continued to the children who were crying, scared, and bruised but still alive.

Thomas overheard one of the little girls whispering to an even smaller girl, "I told you the Riders would come for us, didn't I?"

After calming the children as much as they could, Thomas and Gareth led them out of the town and to the horses. They left the town, with the children riding the horses and Gareth and Thomas walking.

Thomas turned to look at the town behind him and watched as dozens of the risen dead descended on the ruined town to devour the bodies of the Eaters.

## 5.

The city of Ticonderoga was smaller than Thomas had anticipated, but it was still one of the major walled cities in the east and as such, it was civilization. Thomas hadn't seen a real city since he and Gareth left Albany. The walls here were concrete, thick. The Militiamen that greeted them and escorted them to the City Hall were shaved and clean, good and proper soldiers.

People on the paved street stopped and stared at him and Gareth as they walked past. Thomas realized then that they, along with their equally dirty horses, must look like a mess.

When they got to City Hall, the Militiamen took their horses while Gareth hurried up the stairs and inside. Electric lamps lit the building's lush interior. Plush chairs sat in the waiting area.

"What now?" Thomas asked.

"Wait for Mayor Kramer," Gareth said, dropping into one of the chairs.

A few minutes later, a mousy man with a pinched face poked his head out of a door and said to Gareth, "Rider."

Gareth got up and nodded at Thomas. "Come on, kid."

They followed the small man up a set of stairs, along a carpeted corridor and through an open door that led into the mayor's office.

They entered the office and Thomas saw a plump woman wearing glasses sitting behind a polished wooden desk. She was in the midst of devouring a pile of fried chicken.

"Sorry I kept you waiting," she said through a mouthful of meat. "You're the ones that have the package from Albany?"

"Yes, Ma'am," Gareth said, reaching inside his long, dirty coat and withdrawing the small package. He placed it on her desk and she snatched it up in her greasy hands and tore it open like a child diving into sweets. She held the contents of the package up like a prize.

"Oh, I've wanted this forever," the mayor said, tossing the wrapping on the floor.

Thomas couldn't believe what he saw; it was nothing but an old-fashioned music CD. The case was cracked and the picture faded.

*That* was what he and Gareth had risked their lives to bring north. There was no important news in the package, nothing that would improve the lives of people that lived in the cities or in the stick villages. He wanted to reach across the desk and strangle her.

"Mayor, you got anything you need taken down to Albany?" asked Gareth.

"Uh . . . yes," she said. She opened a drawer and handed a wrapped package to Gareth. Thomas briefly wondered what was inside, but then pushed the thought out of his mind. He'd rather not know.

Gareth tucked the package into his jacket, bid his farewell, and then he and Thomas were on their way back downstairs. When they were outside, Thomas said, "You're shitting me, right?"

"I've carried letters full of nothing but jokes. Even chess moves on a couple of occasions."

"That has to piss you off," said Thomas.

"Yup."

"That's all they do?"

"Well, sometimes they send important things, messages and the like. But there's whole lot of nonsense that goes on. People want little things to remind them of the life before . . . even though it don't do a shit's bit of good now."

Thomas and Gareth walked in silence for a few blocks to the barracks where they would spend the night before heading back to the Outlands.

Thomas finally spoke. "I want to stop back in Whitehall on the way to Albany. I want to help them rebuild that wall."

"Sounds good to me, Rider," said Gareth.

# DOWN IN BACK

The land behind the small estate of North Caldwell is hilly and wooded, filled with dark hollows and shrouded glens where streams gush as if they were arteries feeding Mother Earth's blood to the land. Past the gravel driveway that leads to a gray and crumbling house lays an old and twisted dirt road overgrown with weeds and thorn covered berry bushes. It seems to disappear into the forest and leads to a place we called Down in Back.

I take this battered road each Halloween. No matter the weather, despite any prior engagements I may have, I make the short journey. Always, I come alone, and always to the same place, to where a deer runway crosses the road beneath the guard of a skeletal old oak tree with fallen leaves clinging to its roots like some rotting skirt.

I come not because of some sense of duty, and not because of fear. I come to remember, to tend . . . and of course, I come for love.

Even though she is more than ten years in the ground, I still love my grandmother dearly. She is why I return each year, to honor and remember her. She lies with the rest of North Caldwell's dead in the ground Down in Back, waiting for the plate of food that I set out as a remembrance. A silly offering kept up through the years, handed down to me from my grandmother.

She would take me Down in Back with the plate of food as soon as I finished trick-or-treating, before I even changed out of whatever costume I'd chosen for that year.

We would walk the trails, which were in better condition then, and she would tell me about the dead speaking on Halloween, about the veil between the living and the dead being raised on that night. I asked her once what would happen if we didn't come or if we were late in getting there. She looked at me strangely and then smiled. She said, "Never forget the dead, never be late. Terrible things would happen if you are late." I could recall the shiver that went through me when she said that. Those were great ghost stories for a child, but now, some thirty years later, they were just silly superstition. Yet still I come, offering that plate of food every year. This year I was late.

By the time I reached the mouth of the road leading into the woods, it was nearly two o'clock in the morning. Never before had I missed the deadline of midnight, and I had a terrible queasy feeling in the pit of my stomach. It was guilt I suppose . . . certainly not fear. I spent my entire youth wandering the woods around North Caldwell, and I knew there was nothing in the woods that could hurt me.

I began my descent Down in Back with a quick pace. Weeds and briars crept across the road like nests of snakes. When the wind blew along the path, the briars writhed and almost looked as though they were alive. The road wound deep into the woods, past an old tree fort where I played as a child and finally to the little crossroads beneath that oak.

The land looked barren and dead, brown even in the dim light from my flashlight. Crispy leaves crunched underfoot with each step.

I pulled off my backpack and took out the plate of food – cheese, dried meat, and fruit – that I'd carefully wrapped in foil and placed it on the ground in the usual spot. When satisfied that I'd arranged everything just how my grandmother would have liked it, I readied myself to leave. I felt better, even though I'd been so late.

The sound of something creeping through the trees and over the dead leaves suddenly caught my attention. Surely, it was just an animal. Perhaps a possum or skunk, something attracted by the scent of the food I'd just set out.

"Late." The creaking voice came from somewhere behind me.

It was my grandmother's voice. As impossible as it was for me to believe it, I knew it was she, her long dead voice echoing in my mind. I turned, hoping that I would not see her.

She was there though, standing in the roadway wearing her funeral clothes. Much of her graying flesh had rotted away. Her eyes were gone, replaced by small blue flames that looked like flickering candlelight. If not for her voice, I wouldn't have known that it was she who stood before me.

"I told you," she groaned. "Honor the dead. Remember the dead."

"I . . . I'm sorry," I muttered.

"Remember the dead."

Another movement caught my eye, and I saw our old golden retriever, Red, take his place at her side. His once reddish-gold fur was green with mold and missing in several patches. I could see his white ribs clearly. His eyes were the same unnatural blue as my grandmothers. He began to snarl.

The forest around me seemed to awaken then, and I could see more of the walking dead making their way toward me. Uncles, cousins, old pets and loved ones, they began to surround me. Some of them looked freshly buried, while others were nothing but bones. The dead had risen to right my wrong.

"I didn't know," I said. I looked for an escape. "I'm sorry."

They closed in and I could find nowhere to turn, no way to break past them. My grandmother lurched forward and opened her mouth wide.

I understood. They were no longer interested in the plate of food I had brought for their offering.

\*\*\*

From the strange purgatory where I now sleep beneath pungent leaves, dark earth, and a blanket of freshly fallen snow, I think about next year. There will be no one to remember us, no one walking Down in Back to satisfy our needs. We, human and animal, all the dead of North Caldwell, will rise.

# JUNK BOX

## 1.

"Where are last year's tax returns?" Alicia asked, slamming shut the desk drawer. "How do you find anything in that desk of yours?"

Neal shrugged as he always did when his wife got on his case about his tidiness. Other than a little bit of nagging and slight OCD he knew he was lucky to have her. "It's the way I work, babe. Messy desks are indications of creative and productive people. Everyone knows that."

Alicia grinned and tossed a paperclip at him, hitting him squarely on the nose. "You just made that up didn't you?"

"I think I might've heard it somewhere," Neal said, leaning over the desk and kissing the top of her blonde head. "I'll go check the junk box."

"Why would they be down there?" Sighing, she threw up her arms in mock surrender. "Okay, you check your precious box, and I'll go through the papers in the hall closet again. I want to get everything ready for tax season. I hate waiting until the last minute."

It was only the first week of December, but Neal knew there would be no rest until he found those papers. If it were up to Neal, he would have waited until April to start thinking about taxes. Alicia was ruler in these matters though, and he had to admit that life was smoother with her in control

Neal gave his wife a wink and started toward the basement. He was sure the tax papers would be there. Everything ended up in the junk box.

The box, as he and Alicia called it, was nothing special to look at, and that was why it remained hidden in the cellar among the gardening tools and ancient fruitcakes of Christmases past. It was a large cabinet made of pressboard and painted a sickly green. The handles on the warped doors were loose, and the hinges squeaked every time someone opened it.

It was ghastly, but Neal could not part with it no matter how much Alicia pleaded. It had emotional value, he told her, and it reminded him of the early days. The cabinet was the first purchase he had made with Alicia when they moved in together nearly ten years ago. Money was tight back then, and they had needed the extra storage in their small apartment.

They had a house now and more than enough storage space, but the junk box remained like a third member of the family. Despite what he told Alicia, he kept it for more than sentimental reasons. It was special, if hideous to look at. Whenever he lost something, he would check the junk box. Whatever he was looking for, from car keys to laptops, it showed up without fail. It might take a few days, or even a few months, but everything returned to the junk box. He never questioned why or how things found their way into the box. He just accepted and enjoyed the fact that they did.

Neal smiled when he reached the box and grabbed the handles. He threw open the doors with all the gusto of a child opening gifts on Christmas morning.

There, sitting atop the pile of old newspapers, rags, and miscellaneous fuses and plugs, was a large, white envelope. It was torn and dirty, as though it had gone through an ordeal getting into the junk box. On the envelope's front were the words 'TAX RETURN. DON'T LOSE! THAT MEANS YOU, NEAL' scrawled in his wife's handwriting.

Neal laughed and grabbed the envelope. He shut the door, patted the top of the junk box, and uttered a quick thank you before bounding upstairs to gloat.

## *2.*

He pulled his next treasure out of the box two days later. It was a bottle opener with a cartoon picture of a portly Elvis gyrating on the plastic handle. He hadn't seen it since the big barbeque the previous summer. Half of the King's face was missing, and the screws holding the handle together were quite loose. Still, he had his favorite bottle opener back, and that was what mattered.

He was in the middle of cracking open his second beer when the phone rang and he got the news.

"Mr. Kline?" asked a deep voice.

"Yes," he said.

"Mr. Kline, this is Officer Trudeau of the Albany Police Department," Officer Trudeau said. Neal's head spun. The rest of the words were a blur of sound, things that couldn't be true, something about an accident.

"What? She's okay, right?" Neal said. His voice whimpered the words. She couldn't be dead. No, his sweet Alicia could not be dead. She was out buying Christmas presents for her nieces and nephews. No one died doing that. She could not be dead.

"I'm sorry, Mr. Kline."

The full beer bottle slipped from his hand and shattered on the kitchen floor. The beer oozed across the floor and soaked his feet. Neal threw the phone across the kitchen where it clattered against the wall, sank into the lake of beer and broken glass on the floor and wept.

## 3.

The funeral came and went. Dozens of relatives consoled him for his loss, and he didn't even know the names of half of them. He clutched his wife's wedding ring in his hand, barely speaking or making eye contact with them. People feeling sorry for him didn't make him feel any better. As far as he was concerned, life was over if it didn't include Alicia.

His mother stayed with him for a few weeks, making sure he ate and showered. He barely knew she was there, a ghost flitting in to check on him occasionally. She only left when he lied and told her he was doing better, that he would be able to take care of himself.

It was during his first night alone that he heard it. He woke from a nightmare-filled slumber to a persistent and rhythmic scratching like claws scraping against wood.

He let his eyes adjust to the dark room before swinging his legs out of bed. The scraping continued, echoing through the heating ducts.

Rats? Neal mused. If it were rats, they would have to be the size of Great Danes.

He thought about going back to sleep, checking it out in the morning. He could figure it all out later. Then, he felt the cold metal of his wife's wedding ring that hung from a chain around his neck and wondered what Alicia would have him do. She wouldn't let something like this wait. Neal smiled in the darkness and went off to find the source of the noise, just as Alicia would want.

When Neal reached the first floor, he discovered that the sound was coming from the basement. It was still just as pervasive as before, but louder now, more insistent.

Neal quietly opened the door to the basement, eased onto the top step, and shut the door behind him. If there were a raccoon or a cat that had somehow gotten into the basement, he didn't want to give it a chance to reach the upper floors.

He grabbed the flashlight that hung on the back of the basement door and turned it on, so he could see going down the old wooden steps. When he was halfway down, the clawing stopped.

At the bottom of the stairs, Neal swept the flashlight's beam across the cellar floor. No rats scurried, no cats hissed. He didn't see anything that could have been making the sound. Finally, the light came to rest on the box, and the scraping started anew. Dirt fell through the gaps at the bottom of the cabinet doors.

Neal rushed toward the box, understanding what was inside. His magic junk box had returned his lost love.

He tore open the doors, grave dirt spilling onto the cellar floor, covering his feet. He backed away in wonder.

Pale fingers wriggled like worms, pushing away the dirt and splinters from a coffin. A hand broke free and grasped at the air before returning to shovel more dirt away. A leg stretched out of the box at an impossible angle, followed by the crowning of a head covered in clumps of long blonde hair.

"Alicia." Neal sobbed, as he watched the unnatural birth. Part of him wanted to rush to her, to help her out of the box, but animal instinct told him to run. Still, he held the light, trembling and transfixed.

The junk box's latest treasure tumbled clumsily onto the floor and slowly rose to its knees. Neal could see her well now. Lacerations that oozed embalming fluid covered her naked body. Vacant eyes stared at him, and her mouth opened and closed like a fish drowning in oxygen. She started to stand and move unsteadily toward him.

Neal hadn't realized he was backing up until he hit the rakes and shovels lined up along the far wall and knocked them over. The clanging of metal on concrete startled him, and he spun around to see what he had done.

He had taken the light off his beloved for only a second. When he again caught her in the light's beam, he found that she was already halfway across the basement. Her arms were outstretched. He didn't know if she wanted to embrace or strangle him.

She hobbled closer, gaining strength and surety with each step. When she was only a few feet from Neal, she fell forward and he caught her in his arms. He held her close and, for a moment, everything seemed right in the world. Then, her bony fingers dug into his shoulders, trying to rip away the flesh. Her rapidly working mouth that drooled graveyard mud was trying to bite his throat.

He pushed the corpse away, sending her sprawling across the cellar and crashing into the wooden stair railing. She was much faster now though, stronger than she was seconds before, and lurched toward him again.

Neal searched for something to defend himself with, and grabbed a pair of gardening shears that hung on a wall peg. As she reached him again, he brought the blades straight down through her clavicle. This barely slowed her down. She still tried to snap at him. He pushed her away again, dropping his flashlight. The light rolled in a lazy circle, sending light and shadow dancing across the walls.

Unable to see, he picked up a shovel, and swung. A loud crack told him he had found his dead wife's skull. She crumbled to the ground, but he could still hear her hands scraping along the concrete, pulling her shattered body toward him. He brought the shovel over his head and swung with force, repeatedly, until the corpse was still.

## 4.

He was screaming when they found him sitting amongst the strewn remains of his wife, her severed hand in his lap. He was putting her wedding ring on and taking it off, putting it on and taking it off. There was no resistance when the police took him away, and when his trial came he told the truth of what happened, that he didn't dig up his wife's grave and that she returned to him through the magic box. It brings back lost things, he told the judge.

## 5.

The State of New York found Neal to be insane. Each night in his little room at Scarborough Farm, he has nightmares about what happened, and every morning he pleads for the magic box. He tells the doctors if they would only let him have his box, then he would find his lost sanity.

# LURES: A FISH STORY

Let me tell you 'bout the last time I ever went fishing.

You might remember a few years back when all of those severed feet and hands began washing up along Otter Creek. It was all over the papers. The national media got hold and ran with that story, making it seem like we had a gang of Satanists running around the woods of Vermont, hacking folks up and tossing their feet in the damn creek.

Well, I can tell you that it weren't a bunch of devil worshippers. No, it was something else out there…something else entirely.

I had just got off work and was heading out to my fishing hole, hoping I might snag a couple of trout for dinner and make the missus happy. The sun weren't quite down yet – just enough that the dark started easing out over the creek.

Well, I got down to my hole, took a seat on the bank and dropped in my line with a fat nightcrawler wriggling on the hook. I remember that afternoon being near perfect. It was nice and cool…quiet too.

Jason M. Tucker

I sat there for a while without so much as a nibble, and decided to tie on one of my favorite lures. No sooner than I reeled in my line did I see something out of the corner of my eye, something like a glint of light.

I looked up the creek where I had seen the flash. The sun was still on its way down so I figured it was reflecting off an old bottle or something of that sort. I saw the light again, only this time it seemed to be coming from further upstream.

To this day, I can't tell you why I chased after that flash of light, but I did. I got up, grabbed my pole and tackle box, and then went stomping after it like a damned fool. Folks ain't shitting you when they say it was curiosity killed the cat.

I trekked up the Otter for 'bout a quarter mile, maybe less, when the scents of fresh fish, rotten eggs, and something I couldn't quite figure hit me like a fist to the nose. Those smells pulled me, a fool on a string, yanking me onward and over a little hummock where my feet hit something slick. I fell on my ass, snapped my best fishing pole in two, and then slid into a muddy little hollow off the side of the creek.

Didn't have long to feel like a fool though. When I sat up I saw some shit I ain't ever going to forget, and I don't give a rat's ass if you believe me or not. Bodies, all those folks whose feet and hands had been washing up on shore, were partly buried in the mud. Their eyes were missing and their chests were open, gutted, filleted. Some were more rotted than others were, but all looked like something had been chewing on them.

That something gurgled at me from across the hollow.

It was a bony thing, hairless, gray and naked, squatted in the mud. It held a piece of shiny glass in its

89

sharp claws. Shiny mucus covered its skin. The thing's mouth was wide and filled with rows of tiny needle-teeth. The eyes were the worst, dead and dark like a fish. It didn't give a shit what I was. It lured me, wanted to gut me, tear off my useless parts and eat me just like it did to the others. I was food.

The thing inched toward me. I gripped my tackle box and swung it in a wide arc toward the thing's head. The box broke when it connected, sending my tackle into the mud. That gave me a chance to scramble up out of the hollow and back to the woods. I ran to my truck and didn't turn around once to see if it was following.

I can still feel that thing's dead eyes on me; doesn't matter if I'm awake or sleeping. That's why I don't go fishing anymore, why I don't set foot down near those creeks, and why I don't go swimming in Lake Champlain. I know what's down there.

# CONFESSION OF A RIGHTEOUS SERIAL KILLER

Well, tomorrow is the day I walk down that dark and fabled corridor outside this cell. I think I'd be lying if I said I wasn't scared of the death chamber and everything that comes after.

Most people out there with their picket signs marching around this prison say I deserve my fate, and that I deserve burning to a crisp in that chair. I guess the walk to that chair is where most monsters find God and repent. Not me though. I meant everything I did, and I'd still be doing it if they hadn't caught me. That's for damned sure.

I see you cringing already, but you're like most of those folks out there. You know only half the story, you know only the bad parts, and you're ready to condemn me for what you call my sins. That's why I'm choosing to talk to you, so you can write all of it down, the good parts and the bad parts. Put it in your newspaper or your book; put it wherever you want. The people that read and choose to listen will know the truth. I don't expect people to understand completely, but at least they will know.

It all started thirty years, three months, and seventeen days ago. It was winter. Life was good, bordering great. I had a decent job teaching English at the community college. I had a gorgeous wife named Marla and together we had a little boy named Cory. He was a sweetie, with bright blue eyes and a head full of the softest black hair you've ever seen, just like his Mom.

Yeah, life was great back then. God must not like happiness though. He always seems fit to take it from good people.

I remember the day it started, waking to the sound of my screaming wife. I was confused, dazed, unable to figure out what was happening or why she was screaming. She wasn't in the room with me. I pulled my ass out of bed as fast as my brain and body would allow and went to find her. She was in Cory's room, looking down into his tiny crib. It was empty and the window was open. My eyes glazed over and I couldn't breathe. My son was missing, and I stood there like a fucking idiot.

Marla was faster thinking, stronger. She called the police and I went outside barefoot and shirtless but not feeling the cold. I saw tracks leading to and from the snowdrifts beside the open window. The bastard didn't even bother to cover his tracks.

Shortly after, the police came and I showed them what I had found. The prints led to the street and disappeared into the slush, but a team of three bloodhounds found the scent quickly and led the police to the house on the corner.

Come to find out, the cops would have checked that house anyway because it belonged to a sex offender, a child molester. Keep in mind this was a long time ago and there were no laws that required the authorities to let people know there was a monster in their midst.

The house belonged to Marcus Locke. He was the type of guy no one suspected until after the fact. He had barbecues and pool parties where all the little kiddies and their parents were invited. He dressed up like Santa at Christmas and created a haunted house every Halloween. Yeah, he was everybody's pal.

They found my son's tiny body, assaulted and mutilated, roasting in Locke's oven.

As I said before, Locke had been to jail for abusing kids, but I found out that he was released after serving only a fraction of his time. A fucking psychiatrist, no doubt bribed by his bony old rich bitch of a mother, said that his rehabilitation was complete, that he was all better. They let him out, and put him right down the street from Cory.

I'll tell you right now there is no rehabilitation for beasts like Marcus Locke except for death. I can hear the all the politically correct assholes and fat, soap opera watching housewives telling me that I'm wrong. They'll say, "Oh, you're such a horrible, horrible man. No one should die for things they can't help. It's a sickness and they need treatment."

Well, to them, I say, "Fuck you. Wait until it happens to you, when you waddle-walk your dimpled ass into a child's empty bedroom. Wait until your son or daughter, too young to defend him or herself, meets somebody like Marcus Locke. Then come back and tell me that monsters like that don't deserve to die."

My son's funeral was the second worst day of my life. I don't remember speaking to anyone – my eyes had that damned glazed feeling again, and I couldn't even think straight. Perhaps I mumbled a "hello" and a "goodbye," but it was really just a blur. Marla and I drifted apart, as so often happens in times like those. When we should have been comforting one another we simply hated the world. We decided to spend some time apart. The days became weeks, the weeks became months.

Time passed and the day of Locke's trial finally came. I went to the courthouse every single day of that trial. The thing that pissed me off the most was looking at his face; there was no sign of remorse, no sign of emotion at all. I hated him more than I thought could be possible, and I wanted him to suffer in prison, maybe even get a death sentence. Remember, I still believed in the power of the almighty American Justice System at this time.

Locke didn't get the death penalty though. He didn't even get any time in prison because his lawyers, paid for by his mother of course, convinced the jury that he was criminally insane or some such shit. I don't remember the terminology they used. They argued that it would be far more beneficial for Locke to undergo treatment and observation at Shady Valley, a home for the fucked up.

I couldn't believe it. Marla couldn't handle it and went to live with her parents in California. I didn't blame her for going. I knew how hard it was just to live. Running away wasn't an option for me though. I had to retaliate, to fix things as best I could.

I finished out the semester at the college and then tendered my resignation. I told my colleagues that I would be going to Europe to do research for a book. I even promised to send postcards. Traveling to Europe was the last thing on my mind – I just didn't want anyone to report me as missing. I guess I'm getting a bit ahead of myself though.

I loaded the van with groceries, some clothes, some garbage bags, and a few other things that I thought might come in handy for my adventure. Then, I took all of my supplies up to Crane Lake near the New York/Canada border. My parents had a cabin there that they willed to me when they died a few years earlier. It's a nice place, quiet and out of the way. The nearest neighbor is about twenty miles through the woods.

The day after dropping off my gear at the cabin, I headed south again toward Shady Valley and my meeting with Locke.

By looking at it, you wouldn't know that Shady Valley housed monsters. Lush gardens surrounded the facility, which was really just a large brick mansion. A high, iron-wrought gate surrounded the place, but there wasn't a whole hell of a lot of other security. I waited until after dark to try to get inside.

Getting in was easy; the guard at the gate, a elderly man who was more bone than flesh with glasses thick as bottle bottoms set on his angular face opened the gate and waved me through without even checking any identification. There were no orderlies or nurses at the front desk either, but after a little searching, I was able to find a roster of patient names and room numbers. I found Locke's name and went to his room. I figured that if they caught me I could lie and say I was looking for someone that used to work there. Hell, I don't know what I was thinking. I just wanted to get at Locke. I later found out that most of the staff was fired, all having gathered in the common room to watch a baseball playoff game rather than watch the front desk. God bless the New York Yankees. Or the Mets; I don't know who was playing.

I found his door unlocked. Can you believe that? A child molester and a murderer, a bastard that should have been dead or in jail apparently had free run of the facility. I still wonder if his mother's money had something to do with that or if it were just staff ineptitude.

Locke was snoring peacefully, smiling in his sleep. What makes someone like that smile? I wanted to pick up the lamp on the nightstand and crush his skull right then, but that would ruin the fun of it. Instead, I opened the window. It was on the ground floor and I would take him the same way he took Cory.

I bound his mouth, hands, and feet. When he started to come around, I noticed that he seemed drugged out of his mind. Thinking about it now, I figure they probably did it to all of the patients so they wouldn't bother the staff during the game.

After I shoved Locke through the window, I followed and then hoisted him over my shoulder. He was a smaller man than I was, but he was heavy. I hauled him across the lawn and to the parking lot where my van waited.

I figured that when the nurses or orderlies checked his room later, they would think he escaped. It worked because I was never a suspect in his disappearance – at least not until I sent that little present to his mother.

It took most of the night to drive back to Crane Lake. By the time I got there, Locke was starting to come around. I couldn't be sure if he recognized me or not.

I'll tell you right now the things that happened next aren't for the squeamish. But this is the sort of shit that you can't gloss over, not if you want to understand what was in my head and what was in my heart. I was completely sane at the time I did this, and I enjoyed it.

I kept Locke bound so that he was helpless just like Cory was helpless. I looked at him, stared at him for fifteen minutes at least, and he still didn't seem to recognize me.

"Locke," I said to him, "do you have any idea who I am?"

The gag was still in his mouth, but he shook his head that he didn't. I punched him in the face and split his nose like a rotten apple. Watching him bleed was the best I'd felt in a long time and I barely felt the sting in my hand.

I snatched the dirty rag from out of his mouth. "Remember me yet?"

He shook his head, but I thought I saw glint of recognition there. I kicked him and knocked the wind out of him. "Do you remember living on Oak Street in Glens Falls? I know you do."

At this point, I wanted to reach into my back pocket and grab my folding knife and just slit his throat. He deserved a slower death than that though, so I stayed my hand.

His eyes finally lifted and met mine again. A smile creased his blood covered face. "I remember."

I didn't have anything to say to that so I hit him again, square in the nose. That damned smile only left his face for an instant. He seemed to be enjoying his punishment and that infuriated me.

He opened his mouth and spit blood onto the stonework floor.

"Your boy was good. He didn't cry too much. What was his name?"

I couldn't hold back with the knife any longer. I snatched it out of my pocket and unfolded it. In the gray morning light, it almost glowed, like a miniature Excalibur. Locke saw this too, and I finally saw fear register in the monster's eyes.

"Cory," I told him. "My son's name is Cory."

"Yeah, that's right. Cory. Well, Cory was good." As tough and defiant as the bastard still tried to be, I could tell he was scared.

I grabbed his bloody nose, which had nearly turned into a red, mushy pulp, and squeezed. He whimpered and tears came to his eyes. It wasn't nearly satisfying enough.

I pulled on his nose and used the knife to cut deep, wriggling the blade into the cartilage and then sawing through the toughest part until I could yank the remainder free. He screamed, he bled, and it was good.

The thought of my poor son drove me to greater cruelties. I stripped him to his underwear and used an old power drill of my father's to bore holes into his arms and thighs. I made them just the right size for my fingers, which I used to dig and burrow through his flesh like worms. When I grew bored with that, I used a small funnel and poured bleach into them.

It is amazing just how loudly a human being can scream.

Eventually those screams turned to whimpers, so I then pulled aside his yellowed underwear, drilled a hole into his testicles and then cut off his dick. He passed out for a while.

After, I cauterized his wounds with a heated fire poker, boiled his penis and force-fed him his last meal.

When he gagged down his last bite, he began to mumble and whimper.

"Speak clearly," I told him.

"Sorry," he said. "I'm so sorry. Oh, Jesus, please just let me go. Don't hurt me anymore."

I stared at him but said nothing.

"I will never do anything like that again, I swear."

"There is no such thing as rehabilitation."

No one spoke after that. I would wait for him to go to sleep and then poke one of his wounds and wake him. It went on like that for another day or two. I honestly can't remember how long. The only thing I recall from those days is the joy I felt at doing something so wonderful.

I finally finished him off by slicing his throat and letting him bleed to death in front of the fireplace. The romantic in me thinks that I felt his soul pass down to Hell.

I skinned his face – this little mask was a Christmas gift I sent to his mother a few years later – and then dismembered him and buried his pieces in different places deep in the woods. The mask eventually linked me to the disappearance and murder of Locke, but by then I was years gone with a different identity and my righteous career was well underway.

You see, there was no way I could ever return to any semblance of a normal life, not after the things I had done. I was not disgusted with myself and I held no remorse for my actions. On the contrary, I was aching for more vengeance.

It wasn't long before I heard about another case, a bastard quite similar to Locke. He was in Vermont. I went and found him and killed him in a very similar way. His pieces are also buried around Crane Lake if anyone ever wants to go looking.

It kept getting easier, so I kept working at it. Predators were everywhere, preying on women and children. Where the law failed these people, I didn't.

In New Jersey, there was a man named Carlos that killed his wife and then raped his own daughter. She was eight. I cut his eyelids off with a razor and then covered his head with a bag of agitated bees. His face swelled, his throat nearly closed, but I didn't let him die of suffocation. That was too easy. Instead, I cut a hole in his windpipe so he could breathe. I took my time killing him with a corkscrew.

Lest you think of me a sexist, I did eventually take to killing women. Monsters exist even under the fairer sex's skin, and I was the woodsman that would cut down the big bad wolf no matter what guise it used to hide. Do you remember the woman in Ohio? She threw her children off an overpass into rush hour traffic and got off with another insanity plea. I skinned parts of her alive, disemboweled her, and then hung her from the same overpass.

I served as a murderous garbage man, taking out what trash I saw fit. I was not the type of killer that ever had what profilers term a *calling card*. I chose the monsters that deserved to die and then got creative. I suppose that was why it took them so long to catch me. Eventually, they charged me with twenty-eight murders. There are so many more . . . but they can only fry me once, right.

When I first sat down to speak with you, I told you that I was afraid of dying. Now that I think about it, I am not afraid. Heaven has a place for me. There is nothing wrong with what I did. Animals defend their children; they fight and kill for them. We're all animals, right?

Marla wrote to me and told me that she understood what I did. I know Cory understands. Do you? After listening to me, do you understand? I didn't spare you the bloodshed; I told you the truth. What do you think? What would you do? Would you kill the murderer or rapist of your child if you had the chance? I think you would. I pray for your children that you would.

I've finished talking to you now. I'm tired, and I have a big day ahead of me tomorrow. I'm looking forward to the reunion with my little boy.

# RAVEN'S HOUSE

It happened a long time ago, just a few years after I returned from the war. I remember it well, unfortunately. I can still see and smell it....

The woods seemed darker than they should be, as though the sun, still a few hours from setting, didn't want to touch them. Something rotten hid in those trees. Cops get a sixth sense after a while; mine was kicking me in the ass.

Something about that place chilled me. Even with a shotgun in my hands, I didn't want to go down there. I stood on that hill like a fool, cold drops of sweat dripping off the tip of my nose and earlobes and then slithering down my neck like a serpent.

A tug at my belt broke the spell the dark trees held over me. I'd almost forgotten about the little girl, Greta, who I found wandering on that old dirt stretch off Hollister Hill Road, between North Montpelier and Marshfield.

"Sheriff," she said, pointing toward those trees. "That's where it got my brother."

"I told you to stay in the car," I said.

"You'll get my brother?"

"You hop back in the car. There are some deputies on their way here right now. You stay in the car 'til they get here."

She went back to the patrol car, and I started down the hill across the field and into the forest. A trail led into the woods, just as the girl had said, twisting and winding inward. It was silent and darker than I had thought it would be.

The shotgun's stock was slick from my sweat, and I had to stop several times to wipe my hands on my pants. It was then that I heard a sound, a soft cry.

That cry must have given me some courage I didn't know I possessed. I hurried forward, over a small rise. Moss and white sticks covered the ground there, and then I saw the house. It was made of more white sticks, thousands of them, and of flesh, raw and dripping. Ravens sat atop the structure and picked at the meat. The sticks, I soon came to see, were bones of all shapes and sizes. It stank of death.

I felt a rise of vomit but held it back; there was no time to react to the flesh house as the cry was becoming more insistent. I brought the shotgun to shoulder level and moved forward.

At the back of the house, I found the boy, Johann, tied to a stake in the ground. He was whimpering, but he looked unharmed. He gazed up at me.

"She'll come in the dark," he said. "Get us to the light."

I yanked the stake clear of the ground. "Can you walk?"

He nodded.

I held onto his hand as we made our way out. As soon as I could see the sunny field beyond the trees, I heard a screech that made me nearly piss.

We started running.

I heard the thing behind us, breaking through the trees. I chanced to look back once, saw the head of an elderly Native woman perched atop a gnarled body covered in coarse black feathers and moss. The legs ended in hooves and the hands in sharp talons.

"She's a witch," the boy said.

I dropped the shotgun, lifted the boy, and ran out into the bright field. My lungs were on fire and I was seeing spots; I was breathing so hard I didn't even hear my deputies come down the hill for us . . . .

They found nothing – not my shotgun and certainly not the house made of meat, bone, and sinew. The witch, trickster, demon, or whatever it was vanished, or was so good at hiding even hounds couldn't find her.

Of course, I never told anyone what I really saw and neither did Johann and Greta. Who would believe? The deputies thought they were looking for a kidnapper. I never told them any different.

All these years later, when everything is silent and dark, I sometimes hear that screech in the distance, and then I think about what the boy said. She'll come in the dark.

# NIGHT FEEDERS

## 1.

"Aleksy, wake up you lazy boy. It is time. Bernard is already waiting." Gustaw Kasprzak's commanding baritone woke Aleksy from a pleasant sleep and a dream about a girl who lived on the other side of the village.

He wanted to ignore his father's voice, wanted to stay beneath the warm quilt, return to his dreams and see what else might happen with his dream girl. Yet he knew that his father would not let him sleep, not today. With much regret, he opened his eyes, threw off the quilt, and let the cold wake him. Even when there was a fire lit the chill of winter seemed to creep into the old house through the cracked windows and small gaps in the roof. This morning was no different. It was like ice.

Aleksy always thought it miraculous the house stood at all. The little one story hovel was one of the only homes in the village the German bombers seemed to miss during the war seventeen years earlier. Though Aleksy was just a baby at the time, his parents made sure he knew well the terrors of the Nazi reign in Poland, and they made sure he was thankful for all of the things he had, including the ramshackle house.

Still, he didn't like being cold all winter and envied families who had real electric heaters.

"Aleksy," his father said, knocking on the door. "No more sleep."

"I'm awake," he said, swinging his legs out of the small bed, which he'd outgrown two years earlier. The wooden floor was icy and painful on his naked feet. He hurried to the cupboard where he kept his clothes and dressed in the thickest and warmest things he could find. He stuffed a wool hat and thick gloves into his jacket pocket.

After struggling to untangle his curly hair, he headed into the front room. The glow of the dying fire was the only light. His father was there with Bernard Tanski, their neighbor. They looked a very odd pair. Gustaw was reed thin and angular, while Bernard was a bear of a man who always wore a thick beard. Both were smiling and laughing when Aleksy came in rubbing sleep from his eyes. The rest of the household, his mother and sister, were still fast asleep.

"Well," said Bernard, "Look what has risen!"

Aleksy mumbled a hello to Bernard and then sank into the rocker in front of the fireplace. He wanted to absorb as much warmth as he could before heading outside. He eyed the fishing gear sitting next to the door with disdain. The last thing he wanted to do two days before Christmas was go ice fishing. Staying home and reading seemed much more enjoyable.

"You want breakfast before you go?" Gustaw said, gesturing toward a pile of fried potato chunks in the kitchen. "You'll need your energy."

Aleksy pulled himself out of the chair and hurriedly ate his breakfast.

"I hope you are prepared for a walk," his father said, clapping him on the shoulder.

"What do you mean?" The lake where they usually fished was no more than a mile outside of the village. That's where he assumed they were going.

"Bernard it taking us to a secluded spot," Gustaw said.

"Yes, Wilk Lake," Bernard said, as he ran his fingers through his beard's wild tangles. "There will be more fish than we can carry home."

"That's right," Gustaw said. "We'll have carp and perch along with honey cakes for Christmas dinner . . . and then all the way through the New Year!"

"We're going to Wilk Lake?" Aleksy said. An involuntary shiver ran through him. No one went to Wilk Lake. The woods there, and even the lake itself, were full of spirits of the Nazis and the people they'd butchered. Everyone knew that. No one went to Wilk Lake.

"Don't believe the stories you hear," Bernard said, as though he could read Aleksy's thoughts. He placed his hands firmly atop his round stomach. "People are superstitious. Because of their superstition and fear, the lake has grown fat with fish. We can reap the rewards of their cowardice."

"It's so far away though," Aleksy said, hoping he could dissuade the mad fisherman. He looked at his father. "By the time we got to the lake, we'd have to turn around and come home if we wanted to make it back by nightfall."

"We are spending the night on the lake's shore," Gustaw said. He seemed barely able to conceal his excitement. "We will come back tomorrow at midday, our packs overflowing with fish."

The thought of spending a winter night on the shores of a frozen, haunted lake in the middle of a cursed wood was too much for Aleksy. Superstition or not, he wanted nothing to do with the trip. He started to shake his head. "No . . . I can't go there."

"Boy," Gustaw said, gritting his teeth together. He stood up so his skeletal figure loomed over Aleksy. "You are too old to be coddled. You are coming."

That was the end of the argument and Aleksy knew it. His father was an outdoorsman, frightened of nothing, and he seemed to expect nothing less from his son. He finished his potatoes and room temperature coffee in silence, wondering what terrible things awaited him at the lake.

## 2.

Getting to the lake was no easy task. Neither Gustaw nor Bernard owned a car, so the trio had to walk through the silent village. Aleksy saw only a few lights on in the houses they passed. The rest were still dark, awaiting the rising of the sun before the inhabitants would awaken from their slumber. He longed to be back at home, sleeping as everyone else was doing.

When they reached the edge of town, they took an old trail north and deep into the woods. Moving through the snow was difficult, at least for Aleksy. It was close to knee height. His father and Bernard, who were taller by several inches, didn't seem to have as much trouble even though they were carrying the jig poles and the camping gear. Of course, Aleksy thought, they were also accustomed to the outdoors. Gustaw and Bernard chided Aleksy the entire journey for being a superstitious child still afraid of stories meant to frighten babies.

Fortunately, as they entered the deeper part of the forest, the thick interlocking branches above had formed a canopy and kept some of the snow off the ground. This made walking easier, but Aleksy felt a growing dread with every step, expecting to see the specter of a Nazi soldier staring back at him from the woods. The chill he felt in his bones was not only from the winter air.

It was near noon when they reached the lake, but thick clouds that promised more snow continued to hide the sun. Aleksy drank in the tranquility of the lake and surrounding forest. It was silent except for their breathing and the squeak and crunch of snow under their boots.

"Here we are," said Bernard, opening his arms to the sky as he took his first steps onto the iced lake. "Beautiful."

"Enough of admiring the lake, we need to set up camp and gather wood so that we don't freeze to death tonight," Gustaw said. He dropped his share of the fishing and camping gear on the shore and started to clear away some of the snow with a small shovel.

"You're right, you're right," said Bernard. "Aleksy, you can go and gather wood for the fire."

"Where can I get the wood?" Aleksy asked. He was afraid that he already knew the answer.

Bernard laughed and then said, "You are in a forest, where do you think you'll get the wood?"

"Make sure it's dry though, as dry as you can find," his father added. "Get to it, we will set up the rest of the camp and then have lunch when you've brought enough wood to last the night."

Aleksy unburdened himself from the few pieces of equipment he carried, grabbed the small hand axe from his father, and started toward the woods. Each step toward the woods seemed to make the lump in his throat grow larger. He back once to look at his father and Bernard, but they were busy clearing snow from the ground at the lake's edge.

He took a deep breath and plunged into the forest. It only took a few minutes to find the first dead tree. Thankfully, he was still in sight of the camp and could still hear Bernard's bright laugh. It didn't matter how many times Bernard and his father told him that it was silly to be afraid of ghosts and superstitions, he made sure to keep his back to the camp so he could keep an eye on the woods.

After he'd managed to chop an armload of wood from the tree and then bring it back to the camp he'd forgotten about the cold. His father and Bernard had already cleared the ground and began work on a lean-to for shelter.

"Good job," Bernard said. "Now, just bring about twenty more armloads like that and we'll have plenty of wood." He and Gustaw laughed as Aleksy turned back to the forest.

Aleksy ventured further into the woods on his second hunt for wood. It was dark in there, the sun barely able to make it through the thick branches. He always kept the edge of the lake to his left so that he would be able to find his way back. On his third trip, deeper into the woods, he found a deer carcass, ripped apart and picked clean. No doubt in Aleksy's mind that is was wolves that did it. That didn't make the woods seem any friendlier.

With each trip and each armload of wood, his fear of the place seemed to diminish though. Perhaps, he thought, that it was time to stow away his childhood fears and that his father was right. After all, he was seventeen; he was a man now. Men should not fear ghosts, especially ghosts that likely didn't even exist.

On what he hoped would be his final journey into the woods, he crested a ridge almost a quarter mile from camp and as he was coming down the other side he came upon a curious structure. It was made of concrete, partially hidden within an embankment, and mostly covered in vegetation.

Images of Germans came to Aleksy's mind, and he could almost see them in their dark uniforms scrambling into and out of what he took to be a bunker. The place looked untouched, which made plenty of sense to Aleksy. Though the Germans were long gone, the fear that so many people still had of the Nazis was powerful enough to keep them away from the lake for nearly twenty years. After all, it was supposed to be haunted. He suppressed a shudder. Perhaps those childhood fears didn't vanish so easily.

Standing there, simply looking down the steps at the steel door that led into the bunker, Aleksy could feel the old fear mounting in his chest. One didn't tempt a wolf by walking into its den. Still, if he just went inside he could prove to his father that he was a man and that he didn't fear superstitions. That might just keep his father from picking at him for a little while.

Aleksy stood there at entryway to the bunker or base or whatever it was, getting colder by the minute, and trying to work up the nerve to open the door and go inside the place. He took a deep breath of the wintry air, approached the steel door and pulled it open. Stale air rushed out at him.

The meager gray light that peeked in through the forest lit the inner chamber with a dull glow. Inside was a single room with a metal door opposite Aleksy, which he assumed lead deeper into the bunker. The door looked bent, warped near the bottom, as though something from the other side had tried to break through at some point.

Biting the inside of his cheek to help keep from shaking, he stepped into the long and barren rectangular room. The room was not completely empty though. Slumped against the right hand wall were the bodies of seven German soldiers. They were nothing now, just skeletal husks with bits of dried flesh clinging to their bones. One of the soldiers clutched a rosary in his bony fingers.

Aleksy wasn't afraid of them, or of their ghosts. Not anymore. Seeing their bodies somehow made them . . . less. He was curious though.

Aleksy moved closer to the dead soldiers and saw an eighth body seated in a leather chair just beyond the edge of light. He thought that man was an officer because of the decorations on his uniform – although he really didn't know much about how Nazis dressed.

In the man's desiccating hand was a pistol, a Luger Aleksy thought. In the officer's other hand was a piece of paper.

As he looked at the men against the wall, he noticed that each of them had a hole in their skulls. He glanced back to the seated man, and though he couldn't see the bullet wound in the skull, the scene indicated that the officer had shot himself after executing the other soldiers. Staring at them, he wondered what could have happened to bring them to this end.

Aleksy walked toward the officer. He was not a monster now, just dust, leather, and bones. His eyes wandered down to the pistol and the paper the dead man held in his hands. He reached out and pried the paper from the hand. It was a letter written in German, which he couldn't read. He stuffed the paper into his pocket and thought he would have Bernard or his father read it later.

His eyes went back to the Luger. He could take it, bring it back to camp and show his father. It would be a souvenir, a symbol of his banishing the ghost stories of his childhood. He reached toward the pistol, but his hand stopped a few inches short. No. He didn't want that, didn't want to touch it. The letter would be enough.

After one last look at the room, he left the bunker and pulled the door shut behind him, leaving the dead to continue slowly rotting in their cold tomb.

## 3.

When Aleksy returned the camp was set up and a small cooking fire was already burning. He looked at the piles of wood he'd brought back and hoped it would be enough to keep warm through the night. He put the letter beneath his pack and then grabbed his pole and one of the wooden lures that his father carved and painted last summer.

Bernard and his father were already on the lake and sitting on the small folding stools that they had brought with them. Each had dropped their line into the water through the holes they chiseled in the ice.

Aleksy walked out onto the ice to greet them. "You'll never believe what I found!"

"Quiet," his father said. "You'll scare the fish away."

Aleksy wasn't sure whether he believed the fish could hear through the ice or not. In fact, he figured the sound of the hammer striking the chisel and driving it through the ice would serve to scare fish more than a mere voice. He kept to whispers though, trying to appease his father.

"I found something," he said.

"What you need to find is time to chisel through the ice, drop your line and lure, and get a fish," Gustaw didn't take his eyes off the tip of his jig pole.

"I –," he began.

"Fish now, talk later," his father said.

Crestfallen, he grabbed the chisel and the hammer from beside his father's stool and then set off to find his own patch of ice. As he pushed through the fresh snow that covered the lake, he saw several gaping holes covered in only a thin sheet of ice. It looked as though someone had come through and fished recently. He thought about telling his father or Bernard that their secret spot was not as secret as they had thought. They would probably only find another reason to make fun of him though, so he kept silent.

He chiseled his hole, tied the lure onto the line, and then dropped it into the frigid water. His mind wandered back to the bunker and he wondered for a moment if he had imagined it. The musty smell of the bunker still lingered in his nostrils though, so he reasoned that he could not have imagined it. Then he thought about the dead soldiers murdered by their commander. What had they done? What had their last minutes been like?

A sudden shout from Bernard brought him out of his grim reverie.

"Ha!" Bernard shouted again and Aleksy briefly wondered why his father had not told *him* to keep quiet.

"I've got a big one," Bernard said, as he stood up off his stool.

Aleksy could see the jig pole bending nearly in half. He pulled his own line in and hurried over to Bernard, anxious to see what he had caught. By the time he got there, Gustaw was standing next to Bernard with club in hand ready to kill the fish when he pulled it out.

"A carp I bet, must be a monster," said Bernard as he groaned under the weight.

Aleksy looked into the hole and in the black water saw just the back of the fish as it broke the surface. It was a deep red, smooth, and certainly not like any carp that Aleksy had ever seen.

"What was that?" Gustaw asked. It seemed that he had been looking down at the hole as well.

The line pole, unable to take the weight of the fish, snapped in two and Bernard fell backwards onto the snowy ice. He began to laugh. "I told you there were big fish. We need to make bigger holes."

"It didn't look right," Aleksy said, still whispering.

## 4.

The day wore on toward a cold evening lit by a half moon. The trio had only managed to catch a few small fish, certainly nothing as large (*or as strange*, Aleksy thought) as the one that Bernard had nearly landed. It would barely be enough for dinner. Aleksy hoped they would have better luck in the morning. If they didn't, he had a feeling that his father would somehow blame him. Aleksy knew the routine well enough.

He had told his father and Bernard about the bunker, but they didn't seem very interested. The only thing they cared about was getting enough fish, and that had been the bulk of the conversation while they were eating.

Aleksy huddled close to the fire, hoping to escape some of the cold. As soon as his front warmed up, he would realize his rear was cold. He kept heating one side and turning to heat the other until his father told him that he looked like a roast on a spit.

"Sit, boy," his father said. "You make me nervous."

Aleksy sat and stuffed his hands in his pockets to keep warm. When he did, he felt the paper he'd taken from the dead officer. He pulled it out and looked at it.

"What's that?" his father asked, snatching the note away. "A love letter from a girl, maybe?"

"I found it in the bunker," Aleksy said. "Can you read it?"

Gustaw looked at the letter and then handed it to Bernard. "My German is not good."

Bernard moved closed to the fire and squinted at the letter. "The handwriting is poor, but I think I can make it out."

116

Aleksy leaned closer, eager to hear what the letter said.

Bernard cleared his throat and began to read.

"Dearest Anya: If this letter should ever reach your hands, I want you to know that I am sorry and that I love you. I want everyone to know that I am sorry. The world is a wicked place and I've done nothing but to add to that wickedness. The things we have done here, the things we have made. They are unnatural. Foul abominations that God never meant to live. The things we've made, these night feeders, they should not be. Rotted and corrupt, and plucked from the lakes of hell. Yet, I sat here and did nothing to stop it, instead performing my duty for the country I hold dear. They are loose now, all of them. They are coming like a pack of wolves, over the land and through the waters. They can feel my heat. I've relieved my men of their duty and I am alone. They are trying to get through the door. I needed to write this, needed to let you know how truly sorry I am. You need to know that. They are coming for me. I can hear their inhuman language just beyond the door now. I can't bear to look at them again. I will wait for you in the next life even if this letter never reaches you. All of my love, Heinrich."

The camp was silent for a moment and then Gustaw began to laugh, his voice echoing across the lake. "Ridiculous. This is a fiction created by a damaged mind, nothing more."

Bernard didn't laugh and neither did Aleksy. The big man handed the note back to Aleksy. He stuffed it back into his pocket, not wanting to touch the letter. Aleksy was shaking despite the heat of the fire on his face.

"Come now," Gustaw said when his laughing finally subsided. "Bernard, you cannot be as frightened as my little baby boy over there can you?"

"I think we should sleep now and head home in the morning," Bernard said. "The fish here are too small. We will go to another lake."

Gustaw opened his mouth as though he were going to speak, but a tremendous cracking sound that reminded Aleksy of thunder interrupted him.

"What was that?" Aleksy asked.

"The ice breaking," Bernard said. He was already on his feet.

"Something's breaking through the ice?" Aleksy felt the thud of his heart quicken. He wanted to leave. To hell with fishing and to hell the cold. To hell with

118

the bunker and with the letter, and to the hottest part of hell with the dead Nazis. He wanted to go home.

"I said the ice was breaking, that's all," Bernard said. Aleksy could tell by the look in his eyes and the quiver in his voice that the big man was afraid.

"You are children, the both of you," Gustaw said. With that, he stood and walked toward the lake.

When Aleksy turned away from the fire and his eyes adjusted, he could only see his father's silhouette against the white of the snow and ice-covered lake. Beyond his father, Aleksy could see something on the ice, dark shapes slithering toward the shore. They moved fast.

Before Alesky could open his mouth to speak, the things were upon his father, tearing into him. Gustaw screamed and dropped to the ground as one of the things, one of the night feeders, bit into his leg and shook its head back and forth, tearing out a chunk of flesh.

Time seemed to slow for Aleksy. He saw two more of the things begin biting and tearing at his fallen and screaming father. More of them slithered across the lake's surface, and he could see the holes where they were breaking through the ice.

The smart thing to do would be to run into the night, to get as far away from the lake as possible. Aleksy couldn't do that though. His father – anyone – deserved more than to have those things tear him apart. He grabbed the hatchet next to the stack of wood and rushed toward the night feeders, certain it would be the last thing he ever did.

The three that were chewing on his father raised their heads when Aleksy approached, the hatchet held high above his head. The firelight illuminated the creatures. They were almost fish, almost snake, and almost . . . human. The things were as thick as Aleksy's thigh and at least as long as he was tall. They had fins and their gills (at least what Aleksy took to be gills) puffed in and out. Their bodies were sinuous, serpentine. Their heads were wide and wedge shaped with a thick bony ridge along the crest of the head, mouths full of sharp teeth dripping with his father's blood. The eyes gave Aleksy pause though. The night feeders bore human eyes, not the dead eyes of a fish and not the lidless eyes of a snake. They were large and bright, and even in the firelight Aleksy knew the eyes on the night feeders were blue.

He shifted his eyes to look down at his father, whose face and throat were gone, torn away. He brought the hatchet down in a wild arc but managed to cut into one of the night feeders. It let out a shriek and spun its body around, snapping its jaws at Aleksy's wrist. He pulled his hand away just in time. The creature's mouth closed around the hatchet's wooden handle, splintering it.

Something grabbed Aleksy's shoulder and pulled him away from the creatures. His stomach flipped and he let out a small scream, his mind certain that it was one of the monsters. The grip tightened, and Bernard's voice whispered in his ear. "Don't take your eyes from them. Back away."

The other night feeders were on the shore now, clicking and chattering, as though they were speaking to one another. The one that Aleksy had wounded with the hatchet was writhing on the ground, dark blood freezing as it oozed onto the snow. Two continued to feast on Gustaw, snapping and crunching through bone. But five fixed their cold blue eyes on Aleksy and

Bernard. They slithered forward slowly, their fins tucked alongside their sleek bodies.

Aleksy and Gustaw backed away from the night feeders. Aleksy was sure that if he were to turn around they would come at him. When he was younger, one of the neighborhood dogs would do just that, wait for him to turn around and then nip him in the ankles. These were no dogs and they would do a lot more than nip.

The sound of more clicks and chattering began behind them. Aleksy risked a quick glance over his shoulder and he saw two more of the night feeders. The creatures had surrounded them, penned them in as a pack of wolves might do to its prey.

"Run, Aleksy," Bernard said. "Run and don't stop."

The creatures seemed to understand what Bernard had said, for they chose that moment to close in on them. They moved fast, jaws wide and full of gleaming teeth as they rushed forward. Aleksy ran and Bernard followed.

Aleksy was faster and he was soon far ahead of Bernard. A guttural scream echoed through the night, and he knew they had taken Bernard. He could hear Bernard's cries mingling with the sound of ripping flesh. He didn't stop running.

## 5.

Aleksy ran, letting the smaller tree branches smack him in the face and the larger ones tear holes through his clothes and skin. He ran, tears streaming down his face, until his lungs felt as though they were on fire and his head pounded. When he finally stopped, he leaned against a tree and began to shake with cold and fear.

The moon cast very little light through the trees, but Aleksy recognized where he was. He was in front of the bunker. He'd hoped he would be able to find it again because it was the safest place could think of. The creatures were too fast to outrun and there were too many of them.

It would be safe there. It had to be. The night feeders had not been able to break through the door that led deeper into the bunker. He'd seen the damage they did to the door, but they were not able to break through. He would be safe there until the morning, until the night feeders slipped back into black depths beneath the lake.

He closed the outer door tight and sank to the floor, trying not to think of all he had just seen. It didn't seem real. As he sat there in the darkness, his body began to relax and his eyes grew heavy.

## 6.

The sound of clicking and chattering woke him. In the blackness, he could hear the night feeders just beyond the outer door. It sounded as though they were conspiring, whispering to one another. Aleksy kept still and listened, hoping the things would just leave. He had no idea what time it was and no idea how much longer it would be before the sun rose.

The chatters stopped. Maybe they had finally gone, given up the hunt. Aleksy waited another minute before he dared to breathe. At that moment, he felt the impact of one of the creatures slamming into the door. It jarred him, but the steel door held. Another impact came, followed by another and another. Still, the door held.

Aleksy scurried away from the door. He was sure they weren't going to be able to break through, but he didn't want to be so close to them. He backed away from the door until he bumped into the dead officer seated in the chair. The Luger clattered to the floor.

Aleksy fumbled in the dark until he found the pistol, even though he had no idea how to use it. The Luger felt cold in his hand, foreign. The banging on the door continued, the thuds echoing through the bunker. It sounded different now though, and it took Aleksy a moment to figure out why.

The night feeders were no longer only trying to come in through the door that led to the outside. They were also trying to come in through the door that led further into the bunker. The passage beyond the internal door, Aleksy reasoned, must lead to the water. How long would they stay at the doors, bashing themselves against it just to get to him? Hadn't they already eaten enough? The thought of them eating his father and Bernard sent a wave of nausea through him. Would the things even leave at dawn, and how would he even know when it was light out? They were called night feeders, but that could have just been a name, or Bernard could have translated wrong when he read the letter. The only thing he could do was to wait and hope the doors held.

He sat on the floor with the Luger in his hand and waited while the pounding continued for what seemed like hours.

## 7.

Surprisingly, the door that led to the outside, and not the one that led underground, was the one to give out first. The old hinges snapped and the door fell inward. Aleksy could see the gray light of dawn blossom into the room. Dawn . . . but it was too late to save him. They were coming.

The creatures, seven of them, slithered inside now, dark blood running down their raw heads from where they had smashed against the door repeatedly.

Aleksy raised the barrel of the Luger to his temple. He understood now what the officer must have gone through, the fear. He pressed it close to his head and pulled the trigger. It clicked but nothing happened. The gun was empty.

As the night feeders descended upon him, their steely blue eyes unwavering, Aleksy could swear they were smiling.

# THE PATCHWORK BOY

## 1.

Kari saw it out of the corner of her eye, just briefly. The young boy's pale, frowning visage stared at her from an upstairs window in the house next door to hers. As soon as she tried to lock eyes with the boy, he was gone and she wondered if she had imagined him. She had never seen a child over there before. She turned away from her bedroom window and back to her desk, hoping she it was some trick of her mind.

Kari never paid much attention to the dilapidated old house next door. Ever since Mrs. Willow died a few years earlier, the house had fallen into disrepair. The once blue paint had mostly peeled away to reveal gray and cracked boards beneath. No one ever did any upkeep on the yard either. In fact, none of the parade of people that moved in and out of the old house ever did anything to make it any better.

Not that Kari could turn her nose up too much. The house she lived in with her mother her entire eighteen years wasn't in much better condition. Still, the house next door seemed dead somehow.

Kari knew very little of the man who had moved in there the month before, but she didn't think he had any children. She figured she would ask her mother about it when she came home.

## 2.

The aroma of sausage and peppers, along with the heat that emanated from the old gas stove, filled the house. The heat had become so bad that Kari opened a window to let in the evening air and cool down the kitchen.

Fifteen minutes later the rumble of an old Trans-Am signaled that her mother, Marge, was home. Kari was glad to see her mother was sober and in a pleasant mood when she shuffled through the front door. Of course, the smell of sausages and any other heart clogging food always seemed to put her mother, a rather large woman with a rapacious appetite, into a good mood.

"Dinner had better be ready," Marge said, as she dropped her keys onto the cluttered kitchen table.

"About five minutes for the fries."

"Good. I'm starving."

Kari seriously doubted that her mother had ever even been truly hungry in her life.

"Hey," Marge bellowed.

Kari jumped. "What's wrong?"

"Are you trying to heat the outdoors again?" Marge nodded toward the open window. "Shut that damned thing."

"Sorry," Kari said. She reached across the sink to shut the window and saw headlights coming up the neighbor's driveway, cutting through the encroaching gloom. She wanted to watch for a moment to see if a child came out to greet the man.

"Shut the window!" Marge's meaty hand suddenly grabbed and pinched the flesh just above Kari's elbow. She winced and jerked her arm away.

Marge waddled into the living room.

When the food was ready, Kari brought the plate to her mother and placed it on the folding table in front of the sofa, being very careful not to block the view of the television.

"Does the guy next door have any kids?"

Marge shoved a forkful of sausage into her mouth and glared at Kari. "What? No, it's just him. Mr. Gray or some such name," she said, swallowing. She narrowed her eyes and added quickly, "He's too old for you."

Kari shook her head. "That's not why I'm asking. I thought I saw a kid over there."

"Don't go looking over into the neighbor's yard. Keep your nose and the rest of you over here where you belong. You learned that lesson."

Kari bit the inside of her lip to keep from crying. She didn't want to give her mother the satisfaction.

Six months earlier, she had snuck out with a group of friends to see a band play at an all-ages club down in Albany. When she stepped outside to get a breath of fresh air a man had grabbed her, dragged her into an alley around the corner from the club, raped her, and left her crying on the cold ground next to a dumpster.

She kept quiet about it for two months; she had planned to keep it hidden the rest of her life. Then she woke up one morning and went to the toilet with severe cramps. When she looked into the toilet, she saw it in the bloody water. The head and limbs of the fetus were tiny yet defined.

When her mother had found her huddled on the floor there was no sympathy, no trip to the doctor, no love. Instead, Marge reached over, flushed the toilet, and then yanked Kari up by the hair and began screaming at her. That was just how Marge dealt with things, and that was why Kari hated her so.

## 3.

After finishing the dishes, Kari took the garbage out to the trash bin on the side of the house. There was a light drizzle, and it seemed far too cold for late March.

A faint sound caught her attention as she headed back to the house. At first, she thought it might just be raindrops as they hit the shingles on the roof. The sound was too deliberate though, and it was coming from the neighbor's yard.

She made her way to where she could see into the lot next door. The tapping grew louder. It was coming from the neighbor's basement window.

Kari, staying well within the confines of her own yard, knelt down to peer through the window as best she could.

She saw the boy's face again, only this time he was smiling. Kari smiled back.

She wondered if Mr. Gray had abducted the child or if her mother was simply mistaken and he did indeed have children. She also wondered how the boy had known to tap on the window just as she was heading to the trash. Had he been waiting? Did he watch her and know that she took the trash out at this time every night?

The boy continued to smile and then his face dropped out of sight. Kari stood up and went back inside, still wondering about the child.

She spent several hours lying awake in her bed. It wasn't until she committed herself to learning more about the boy and making sure that he was safe that she was finally able to drift to sleep filled with dreams of pale children and bloody fetuses.

## 4.

When Kari woke to make her mother's breakfast the next morning, it was pouring rain outside. She hurried downstairs and when she prepared the omelets, she forgot to add onions. Her mother reminded her of how important onions were with a banshee screech that shook the walls.

As soon as Marge left for work, Kari looked into the neighbor's driveway. Mr. Gray's van was gone, which meant the neighbor's house was empty except for the child.

Kari slipped on a windbreaker and headed into the backyard without a clue as to how she was going to try to contact the little boy. She stood in the backyard for a few minutes, contemplating whether she should just knock on the door or maybe rap on the basement window as the boy had done the previous night.

As she stood there pondering, the child appeared and grinned at her from a ground floor window. She smiled and mimed for him to open the window. He seemed nervous but reached forward and opened it.

"Hey there," Kari said. "You live next door now, huh?"

The boy nodded. Kari could still only see his pale face hidden in the shadows of the darkened house. His hair was blond and wispy, and his eyes were dull amber.

"What's your name?" Kari asked. "I'm Kari."

"I know your name," the boy said, staring. His voice barely rose above a whisper. "I hear that woman yelling it sometimes. Is she your mommy?"

Kari nodded. She had always wondered if the neighbors could hear her mother's rants. Amazing that no one had ever thought to call Child Services in all the years of abuse she suffered. The concept of 'love thy neighbor' seemed lost on the denizens residing in the town of Silver Point. They liked to gossip, but they wouldn't raise a hand to help.

"What's your name?" Kari asked again.

Confusion seemed to cross the boy's face. "I don't know. I've had lots I think. Now I'm just . . . ."

Something was wrong with the child and Kari was determined to find out what it was. She could not leave him to fend for himself, as she'd had to do her whole life. Taking a breath, she stepped across the invisible barrier that separated her yard and the neighbor's.

"What are you doing?" he asked.

"I want to talk to you some more," she said. "Are you okay?"

"Are you here for me?" the boy asked, his eyes widening.

Kari neared the window and the boy inched away. "Do you need help? I'll help you."

"I don't think you can," the boy said. "He won't let you."

Jason M. Tucker

"You mean your daddy?"

He shrugged. "I guess that's what he is. That's what he says he is."

The boy suddenly looked as though he were about to cry and turned and ran into the dark house.

Kari's eyes darted around the yard to make sure that none of the nosy neighbors was outside or peeking out their windows. When she was satisfied that no one was watching, she hoisted herself up through the window where she tumbled headfirst onto the hardwood floor.

"Stupid," she muttered as she clambered to her feet and let her eyes adjust to the room's murkiness. The room into which she fell held an old and ratty sofa that made the furniture in her own house look positively ritzy by comparison. A rocking chair lay broken near the fireplace. A shattered lamp lay on a dusty end table. Dampness seeped through the house.

"Hello," Kari said, calling out to the boy. "Let's go over to my house." She wanted to get him out of there. Even if he was the man's son, there was no excuse for leaving a child his age – he couldn't have been more than eight or nine – home alone. It was dangerous, neglectful.

"I don't know if you want to be here," the boy called from somewhere in the dark.

"I don't think it's safe for you," Kari said, trying to follow the sound of the boy's voice. Something on the ground caught her attention. It was a chain. Her stomach knotted. The man kept the boy chained.

"It's really not safe for anyone here," he said.

Kari followed the voice and the chain. They led to a closet in a short hallway just off the living room. She reached toward the closet door and opened it.

131

The smell of old, damp clothes and rotten wood rushed out at her. In the dark, she could barely see the small child huddled on the floor. She reached a hand forward slowly as not to frighten him. He looked up at her and his hand, small and cold, grasped hers.

When he stepped into the hallway's dim light, she saw him fully. He was dressed in blue shorts and a grimy white t-shirt. His face, which she had seen before was like that of any young child, round and soft. That was where the similarities to a normal child ended, however.

Stitches, thick and black, encircled his neck and closed what appeared to be a fresh wound. At his left elbow, more stitches attached a forearm and hand, a replacement that obviously did not belong to the boy, as they were those of a larger African American child. The right leg was several shades darker than the boy's pale face. It was also about four inches shorter than the left leg, which Kari thought must give him a severe limp. At the end of the longer leg was attached a shackle and chain. Scars and hastily stitched wounds covered the patchwork boy's arms and legs. Only his face remained unblemished.

"Don't be scared," he said. His eyes pleaded.

"I don't understand how . . . ," she said.

"He put me together from dead pieces he collects," the boy said. "He used stitches and special words to make me."

"You can't *be*."

"He uses stitches and words like magic," he said. "Now I'm here with him forever while he tries to make me perfect. He hurts others to do that, but it's so I'll be perfect."

Kari's head spun. She didn't understand what he meant by words and stitches and she didn't care; she had to get him out.

"Do you have a phone here?" she asked, thinking about her own cell phone that lay useless atop the dresser in her bedroom.

The boy shook his head.

"I'll go to my house and call the police," she said.

"Don't leave. He's going to come back," the boy said.

Kari hugged the child. He was cold and smelled sour, rotten.

"I won't leave you. But we've got to get the chain off your foot so you can come next door with me," she said. She looked at the shackle and chain attached to his ankle. "Do you know where there are any tools? I need something to cut the chain."

"I know where he keeps saws," the boy said. He pulled himself from Kari's embrace and scurried back down the hall and through the living room, the chain dragging behind him. Kari followed him back through the living room, down a hallway and through an open door that led down a set of creaking stairs into the basement.

## 5.

A single overhead bulb at the bottom of the stairs lit the basement. A chain dangled from it that was low enough for the child to reach.

There was a window on each side of the basement, and Kari could see a milk crate beneath the window where the boy had watched her last night. In a corner of the basement was a nest of blankets, storybooks, and toys. The air was thick and stank of rotted meat.

"This is where you stay, isn't it?" Kari said, her eyes scanning the basement for tools of some sort.

"He keeps everything back there," the boy said, pointing toward the rear of the basement.

Kari could see a makeshift wall made of plywood with a large hole cut out for the door. She didn't want to see what was beyond that gaping hole. "That's where the saws are?"

"Yup," the boy said. Then he added in a whisper. "I don't like going in the Gutting Room. It hurts."

"Don't worry, I'll get the saw," Kari said. The last thing she wanted to do was go into that place, the Gutting Room. She didn't seem to have a choice though. "Is there a light in the room?"

"Yes. It's like that one," he said, pointing to the overhead light at the bottom of the stairs.

She moved quickly, wanting to get the whole ordeal over as soon as possible. As soon as she reached the doorway, she reached forward and found the pull chain for the light.

The first thing that struck her was the orderliness of the little room. Hooks on the walls held a variety of different saws and blades. Metal trays along one wall held other tools. Most of them looked like medical instruments, scalpels, suturing needles and the like. A large freezer occupied one corner of the room, and Kari tried not to think about what it held.

In the center of the room was a metal table with leather straps. It reminded Kari of an operating table.

A circle of yellow paint on the floor encompassed the table. Inside the circle were letters and symbols that seemed to glow the longer she looked at them.

A cold, small hand suddenly grabbed hers. Her breath caught in her throat and she pulled away. She looked down at the patchwork boy who frowned up at her.

"You won't make it in time," he said.

Kari nodded and chose a hacksaw from the wall. She ushered the boy from the room and shut off the light.

She pointed to the blankets. "Have a seat and we'll get this off of you."

He eased himself onto the mound of blankets.

"How come you never got my attention before?"

"I've only been alive for a little bit," he said. "I didn't know if it was a good idea. Now I think it was."

Kari began sawing away the chain.

## 6.

The child talked the whole time she worked on cutting through the chain, telling Kari that she might want to hurry, telling her that he was several boys mashed into one perfect boy. He had bits of memory from all of them, but he didn't know who he really was.

"We're done," she said finally, dropping the chain and the saw onto the floor. Her hands were raw and bloody.

"Listen," whispered the boy. His eyes grew big and he grabbed onto Kari. "He's back."

Kari heard the sound of a door opening somewhere in the house above and someone's feet walking across the creaking upstairs floor. Kari grabbed the boy's hand and pulled him toward the window that faced her house. The hinged window swung inward. Kari lifted the child and pushed him through the window.

"Run to my house," she said. "I'll be right behind you."

"He'll get you," the boy spun around on his knees in the mud and grass. "He'll make you like me."

Behind her, she could hear the basement door opening and the man hurrying down the stairs.

"Just go," she said as she hauled herself partway out of the window.

The boy didn't move. His amber eyes ate into her. He leaned forward and began whispering. "I have to tell you something. He wanted me to see if you would come. If you came to help me, he knew you would be worthy of the gift. You will be part of the family now too."

"No . . ."

Strong hands suddenly grabbed her ankles and yanked. She grasped at the crabgrass and weeds in the yard but couldn't find purchase. Her jacket rose up and her bare stomach scraped along the bottom of the window ledge as Mr. Gray pulled her inside.

Kari struggled and managed to free one of her feet from his grip by slipping out of her sneaker. She used her heel and slammed it into what felt like his face. A growl of rage erupted from behind her and the grip on her other ankle loosened.

As she resumed crawling through the basement window, the boy crouched and scrambled toward her. He pushed on her shoulders so she slipped backwards and deeper into the basement.

"No," Kari screeched as she fought against the child. From behind, Mr. Gray's strong hands renewed their grip on her ankles. With one strong pull, he

136

dragged her through the window where she fell to the floor. The air rushed out of her lungs; she whimpered and grunted trying to get a breath.

Mr. Gray turned her over and lifted her into his arms. His face was pale like the child's, but his eyes were a brighter shade of yellow and they glowed fiercely in the dimness of the basement. She turned away from his strange eyes, still struggling for breath, and saw the patchwork boy crawl through the window. The child was grinning at her.

"Get the table ready, and I'll start making a sister for you," said Mr. Gray, his voice silken and slippery.

Kari struggled, but Mr. Gray's strong arms held her fast.

"Hush," he said, as he brought her into the Gutting Room.

## 7.

"She never even put out a missing person's report on you. She thought you left with some boy. She still says terrible things about you," Mr. Gray said. "You see why we took you now?"

Kari nodded. The pain was not as great as it had been when she first came to life a little over a month ago. The stitches were healing nicely and the other girls' parts fit her well. Unlike the boy, whom she had taken to calling William, she had full memory of her original life. She remembered mostly the terrible things, pain caused by her mother.

"You want a new mother, a better mother, don't you?" asked Mr. Gray, his yellow eyes shimmering.

Kari nodded.

"Then you must get rid of the old one first. Cleave your past," he said, handing her a large knife from the Gutting Room wall. "Then we'll make a new mother and be a whole family."

Kari nodded again and took little William's hand. Together the patchwork boy and the patchwork girl ascended the basement stairs with preternatural grace and speed, their amber eyes helping them to see in the near darkness. They headed toward her old mother's house for one final visit.

Jason M. Tucker

# MEAT CITY

## 1.

It was almost time to kill a man.

The world began to take on the lovely blue tinge it always does in winter, just as the sun begins to dip below the horizon and cast those long and twisted shadows across the land. As darkness slowly fell over the city, a powdery snow began to fall along with it, coating the urban landscape in a cleansing layer of white. The snowfall started gently enough but the flakes quickly grew larger and thicker, falling faster and multiplying.

Granger Black sat in his rental car and watched the snow, trying not to think of the cold that bit at his fingers even through his skintight gloves, trying not to think that he still had hours to wait. The dance of snowflakes against the red, green, and blue Christmas lights decorating houses had a hypnotic effect on him.

He had grown up in the deserts of California. The only time he'd seen snow was during the one winter when his uncle and grandmother had taken him to Big Bear. He remembered the blue corpselike hue of the snow at sunset, just as the world looked now. He shivered at the thought of that winter trip, of his uncle, and it had nothing to do with the snow.

As much as he disliked the snow, it would make the kill and the getaway even easier. If the storm were large enough and if it kept people inside over the holidays, no one would even find Paul Castillo's body for at least a week. Not that he figured anyone would even be looking for Castillo, not on Christmas or any other day. He was a man without anyone. Granger was reasonably sure that no one gave a rat's ass about whether Castillo was alive or dead. That was the one thing that Granger had in common with Castillo. That was the only thing.

Of course, if the storm were too big then he'd end up stuck in Chicago along with Castillo's body. He had hoped to be back in California by tomorrow, Christmas day. Back home to a large beach house where there was no one waiting for him. At least it would be warmer.

Granger fiddled with the radio until he found a station that was playing Christmas songs. He leaned back in his seat, watched the snow, and hummed along as Brenda Lee's *Rockin' Around the Christmas Tree* poured from the car's stock speakers.

Granger didn't necessarily *like* killing. He was simply good at it. He had the patience of a saint, albeit a vicious saint, when it came to waiting for his prey; he had the steady nerves that it took to do the job; and most important, he had an ability to dissociate himself from even the nastiest of wetwork. Murder paid the bills. Hell, it did more than pay the bills; it allowed him to have luxuries he never thought possible when he was a little boy growing up in that decrepit Barstow trailer park that baked beneath the California sun and living with a daft grandmother and an uncle he wished never existed.

Grandmother Black had always told him that if he wanted to go places in life he had to find something that he was good at, something that no one else wanted to do. She said that when you found a job that no one else wanted, you stick with it. People would pay good money to have it done. Of course, Grandmother Black had no idea that the dark haired, blue-eyed cherub she rocked to sleep every night would grow up to become a highly paid butcher.

*Jingle Bell Rock* from Bobby Helms followed Brenda Lee, and the Beach Boys followed that with *Little Saint Nick*. It was just about enough to put a little of the holiday spirit into him, to make him forget that he was going to gut someone in a few hours.

Some jobs were easier than others were. Killing Castillo would be one that Granger didn't mind. Hell, he probably would have done it free of charge, a Christmas gift, if the client had asked.

Castillo was a child molester and to Granger that was the worst kind of evil, something that he didn't mind purging from the world. He knew that might sound strange coming from someone that killed for money, but there was a difference. Castillo had raped the client's daughter, but his case never went to court because Castillo fled. His client wanted revenge, reasonably so, and Granger was more than happy to oblige.

As soon as the house lights went out on the quiet little street, he would head down the block, slip into the small two-story house that Castillo rented, and do the deed.

He figured that most people on the street would turn in early to get ready for whatever festivities they had planned for the next day and all the children would be in bed early since they didn't want to piss off Santa. No child in his or her right mind would want to run the risk of relegation to the naughty list so close to the big day. As soon as they were all asleep with visions of sugarplums dancing in their heads, he would start work.

He watched as an oversized SUV pulled into a driveway several houses down from Castillo's place. A heavyset man stumbled out of his car dragging what looked like a suitcase behind him. He lurched toward his house on unsteady feet. The heavy man stopped and swayed, vomited onto his own large gut, and then lurched forward again. The man stumbled and limped into the house.

The street was once again serene and still.

Granger looked at his watch. Another hour, maybe less, and it would be time to get to work.

## 2.

It was cold as hell in the old warehouse, and the single fire barrel could do nothing to stave off the chill. Snow poured in through some of the holes in the roof, making neat piles on the concrete floor.

At least it was out of the wind, Preacher thought, as he tossed more newspaper onto the fire. At least there was that. He tried to warm his hands over the flames; he rubbed them together and tried to forget the cold . . . nothing doing.

"Hey," a voice echoed from the shadows at the far end of the warehouse.

At first, Preacher thought it was cops come to rouse him from the building, but he quickly recognized the voice. It was Junebug. He was the only real friend Preacher had on the streets. Preacher hoped he was coming back with good news or at least something to eat. He hadn't had a bite to eat since yesterday morning.

Though they had dealt with similar blows in their life, Preacher and Junebug were about as different as two people could get. Preacher was a black man, tall and slender as a flagpole, born and raised in Chicago. He had a degree from Illinois State University, but all that little piece of paper got him was a job as a factory manager until the place went under a few years ago. His wife and son had left him and moved to Jersey not long after. How old was Sammy now? Sixteen sounded about right. He hadn't seen nor heard from Sammy or the ex in almost four years. He couldn't blame them. He didn't have anything to give.

Junebug was a white man except for the red streak that ran across the back of his neck. He was built like a fireplug and not much taller. He'd dropped out of high school back in Fouke, a place that Preacher thought was somewhere in Arkansas. One of Junebug's less than endearing qualities was that he never knew when to keep his mouth shut.

No matter whom they were, no matter where they came from, each was the only thing the other had now. They were friends by necessity and chance rather than by choice. That was fine by Preacher. Even with his big, foul mouth, Junebug was what you would call *good people*.

"What's the good news?" Preacher asked, as Junebug finally made it to the fire barrel.

"There ain't much good news," Junebug said. He put his hands over the fire. "Shelters are full up, naturally. Every fucker in the city is trying to get into one of those places, get out of this cold."

"Sort of how I figured it would be," Preacher said. He grabbed another piece of old newspaper and began twisting it to throw onto the fire. He did his best to hide his disappointment. He had truly hoped that Junebug would come back and tell him that one of the shelters had a few beds left. He remembered last year at Christmas when he and Junebug had both gotten beds for a whole week and hot meals to boot.

God, he loved the holidays. It seemed like everybody was willing to do just about anything for street folks like him. Of course, that good spirit only lasted a few weeks out of the year. Everyone was afraid that Jesus was watching and judging, and no one wanted Jesus to think that he or she were an asshole. It made Preacher chuckle. Jesus Christ, indeed.

"I did manage to score us some goods though, my man," Junebug said, smiling. "Merry Christmas." His missing teeth made him look like a jack-o'-lantern when he smiled. The orange glow the flames cast on his face served to strengthen the impression.

Preacher hoped it was food. Junebug was a drinker, and whenever it was his turn to go scrounge up some grub while Preacher guarded their shelter there was always a fifty percent chance that he was going to come back with booze rather than something to eat.

Junebug reached a dirty hand into his tattered coat and withdrew two wrapped deli sandwiches and three full packs of cigarettes.

Preacher felt himself grin, an unfamiliar feeling. Food and that many smokes on the same day were damn near a miracle. This might be an okay Christmas after all.

"Where did you get them," Preacher asked.

"Got the sandwiches down at the shelter in Lincoln Park and they said we could come back tomorrow for some more, probably even get a hot meal since its Christmas and whatnot. I tried to get a couple extra, but they wouldn't have it," Junebug said. He handed Preacher a turkey on wheat.

"What about the smokes?"

Junebug did his best impression of a carved Halloween pumpkin again. "Let's just say that someone down at the mini mart wasn't paying too close attention so I reached over the counter and liberated them."

Preacher frowned. He didn't like stealing, but he knew as well as anyone else that you had to take the opportunities you got, even if that meant ripping someone off from time to time. He opened his sandwich and took a bite. Just like heaven.

"Heard some weird shit's been going on too," said Junebug through a mouthful of meat and bread. "Something crazy been happening out at O'Hare."

"What kind of crazy?"

Junebug shrugged. "Hell if I know. I heard people down at Lincoln Park talking about folks coming off the plane all sick, like they got food poisoning or something. I don't know about food poisoning, but I heard that they wanted to keep people to check them out . . . what do you call that?"

"Quarantine," Preacher said.

"Yeah, right. But people weren't having that this close to the holidays, some of them just left, busted right out of there or some such shit."

"That right?"

"Yup," Junebug said. "I bet some idiot brought some bug back from China or France or one of them foreign places. That happened a few years back. You remember that?"

"Yeah, I remember something about that," Preacher said as he continued to chew, even though he didn't know what in the hell Junebug was babbling about. What happened all the way over at O'Hare didn't concern him. All he wanted to do now was enjoy his dinner and then have a nice cigarette to help wash it down. He might even smoke two.

He took another bite of his sandwich and began to chew when a very literal hell started to break loose.

## 3.

Holly chewed on her lip and watched the flannel wearing man sitting in the corner booth. He was hunched over and gripping his stomach. She hadn't even seen him come into the diner. When she got back from her break five minutes earlier, he was just there. He looked like death, pale and shaking. A suitcase with airport tags sat next to him.

That was just great. It was flu season, he was sick as hell, and he just had to choose the Fry Shack for some artery clogging fried meat before running home. With her luck, she would catch whatever bug he had and be sick for Christmas. Her mother would find a way to blame her for it.

Ah, she thought, the glamorous life of a waitress at a crappy little diner. She wondered who would play her in the movie and then sucked in a deep breath, put on her fake smile, and hurried to the table. Better to get it over with fast.

"Hi there," she said, still wearing her ear-to-ear smile. The closer she got to the booth the more it smelled like vomit. God, she hoped he would just order coffee and leave. "What can I get for you this evening?"

Flannel Man looked up at her with vacant, hollow eyes. He stared through her not at her. He sniffed the air twice, gently moving his head from side to side as if he were trying to catch her scent.

"Um . . . are you feeling okay?" she asked.

His eyes rolled into the back of his head for a moment and then came rolling back like a slot machine. They were darker now, all pupils and no iris, still staring through her. Before she could look away from the dead shark eyes, a thick, black tongue covered in some kind of mucus, lolled out of his mouth.

Holly took a step back. What was wrong with him? Nobody had a tongue like that. She took another step back and another until she bumped into the counter.

"Hey, Mitch," she called, careful now not to take her eyes off the booth.

Mitch was the diner cook. He wasn't big and he wasn't burly. In fact, he was just the opposite of big and burly. He was scrawny, scraggly, and he was about fifteen years Holly's senior. He was the only other person in the diner though and Holly didn't want to be alone with the black tongued weirdo.

Mitch came out from the back. Holly could see him out of the corner of her eye wiping his hands on his grease-stained apron. "What's up?"

Holly nodded toward Flannel Man. "There's something wrong with him."

"Like what?"

"Hell if I know, but it ain't good," Holly said. She took her eyes off the sick man for just a moment and looked toward Mitch.

Mitch gave a *what-do-you-want-me-to-do-about-it* shrug.

"He's creeping me out. Can you just ask him to go or something?" Holly tried to smile at Mitch. That was usually all it took. He sighed and walked over to the booth. Holly could see the large kitchen knife tucked through the back of his belt. The knife was part of Mitch's nightly ensemble. Diner work in this part of town could get ugly late at night. For that matter, anywhere in Chicago could get ugly late at night.

Flannel Man's blackened tongue slid back inside his mouth, leaving a trail of slime across his lips. He turned his dead gaze away from Holly and toward Mitch.

"Look, man, you're going to have to leave. We're closing up shop pretty soon," Mitch said.

Flannel Man said nothing, but Holly thought she could hear breath creaking out from between his lips.

"You need me to call you a cab or something?" Mitch said. "You need a ride home?"

Again, Flannel Man said nothing.

Mitch turned his head back toward Holly and spoke. "Can you believe this guy?"

The man was now starting to rise, slow and unsteady. The tongue slipped back out of his mouth and he licked his lips.

"Something isn't right," Holly said. "Come on and let's just call the cops so they can –"

The man grabbed hold of Mitch and sank his teeth through the white t-shirt and into the meat of his shoulder. Mitch let out a howl and spun away from the

148

man, tearing away a large chunk of flesh from his own shoulder in the process.

"Fucker bit me!" Mitch yelled. He reached behind his back with his good arm and pulled out the knife. "Call the cops before I kill him."

Flannel Man chewed on the meat from Mitch's shoulder, blood and stringy bits of flesh dribbling down his chin. The dead, black eyes continued to stare.

Holly stood stock still, not daring to move, not believing what she had just seen. She couldn't even take a breath and her feet felt weighed down with stones. Who would bite someone like that? Who would bite someone *period*?

"Holly!" The sound of Mitch's voice started to break her out of her reverie. She could see Mitch, arm bleeding, holding the knife in front of him and squaring off with the man. Flannel Man didn't seem to care; he continued to chew. Still, Holly's feet wouldn't move. The world seemed awash with gauze that coated her vision. Her stomach rolled and she thought she was going to be sick.

Flannel Man lunged, impaling himself on Mitch's blade, not stopping, not squirming, not trying to get away, not caring about the blade, just coming closer, pushing himself deeper on to the knife, getting closer, his mouth opening and closing, his black tongue wagging and wriggling like a worm.

Mitch let go of the blade and started to back away. Too slow. Flannel Man's hands shot forward, wrapped around Mitch's throat, and then squeezed.

Holly watched helplessly as Mitch tried to push away, but the man seemed too strong. Mitch gasped and Flannel Man pulled him closer, closer, until their faces were almost touching. Flannel man opened his mouth wide and bit down on Mitch's cheek just below the right eye, bit down and began *chewing* on Mitch's face. Mitch grunted and tried to push Flannel Man away.

Holly finally found the will to move. She ran, burst through the doors of the diner and into the dark snowy night. She didn't turn back, not even when she began to hear Mitch scream.

## 4.

Granger hadn't seen anyone in the past hour. The street was devoid of life and the only movement came from the ever-falling snow and the twinkle of lights. It was time.

He stepped out of the car, shut the door as gently as he could, and then walked along the sidewalk with his hands tucked in the pockets of his coat until he reached 811 Johnson Street. The lights inside were off, except for the soft glowing pulse emitted from a television in what Granger assumed was the living room.

He crept around to the back of the house and up the steps of the back porch, slowly as not to make a sound. The snow was still pouring steadily so he didn't worry about leaving tracks.

According to his client, Castillo, who was living under a false name, didn't have any type of security alarm, and he didn't own a dog. He tested the door. It was unlocked; he wouldn't even need to break the glass or pick the lock. Between the snow and the easy entry, it looked like fate and fortune were smiling down at him. He knew not to trust either fate or fortune though; they were fickle things that would turn on you as soon as they had the chance.

He turned the knob slowly and pushed the door open inch by inch. When the gap was wide enough, he slipped inside and closed the door behind him. He stood in the darkness for several minutes, barely breathing, letting his eyes adjust.

The back door had led him into the kitchen, which was a wreck. Dishes piled high into precarious stacks filled the sink and black shadows scurried across the floor – *rats*, Granger thought. Pizza boxes stacked four deep littered the kitchen table and atop those were containers from some Chinese takeout joint. The place smelled sour and rotten like body odor and old milk. To say the place was a sty would have been understating it.

A cough from somewhere else in the house caught Granger's attention and caused the hairs on the back of his neck to stiffen. It wasn't a man's deep cough; it sounded like a child and it sounded as though it came from the second floor.

The cough came again, soft and, yes, feminine, but Granger barely had a chance to register the sound before he heard a voice coming from the room adjacent to the kitchen.

"Quiet, if you know what's good for you, little bitch. I'll gag you, you don't shut up," the man said. His voice was nasal, whiny, and there was a slight Mexican accent.

Right street, right house, and the right accent – it had to be Castillo. It also sounded as though he had company that didn't want to be there. This changed things. He couldn't just kill Castillo and then leave whoever was in the house there to rot. Castillo had likely bound the person – a young girl if he knew Castillo's preferences. The kid would starve or freeze before someone found them. If he freed the girl, she would be able to give the police a damned fine description of Castillo's killer. He wasn't about to leave some poor kid trapped in the house with Castillo either. He might be a murderer, but damn it, he had a conscience.

The night was turning to shit damn quickly.

A thousand scenarios ran through his mind as he tried to find another option. It turned out that he didn't need to choose – Fate, the diabolical old bitch, chose one for him.

Castillo stepped through the swinging door and into the kitchen. He flipped on the light and his eyes widened when he saw Granger standing there. Castillo was wearing a Santa hat and bright red jacket, but he was devoid of pants and naked from the waist down. Obesity had shriveled and hidden any sign of a penis.

Granger saw the fat man's hand reaching toward a filet knife on the cluttered counter. He was faster than Castillo was though and he had the advantage of surprise on his side. He closed the distance between himself and Castillo in a fraction of a second, his left hand trapping Castillo's hand against the counter before it could reach the knife. He simultaneously smashed Castillo's jaw with a roundhouse delivered by his right elbow, spinning the fat man's head.

Castillo grunted and whimpered, but he didn't go down. He outweighed Granger by at least a hundred pounds, and he started to push his bulk into Granger.

Granger held ground for a moment as Castillo pushed and then, still holding onto Castillo's hand, he twisted his body and let the fat man's mass and momentum carry him forward and spill onto the dirty linoleum floor. He felt a satisfying pop as Castillo's wrist snapped.

Castillo cried out, and the only thing Granger could think of was that he needed to shut him up before someone called the cops. Granger kicked Castillo in the face until he was unconscious and then he reached into his jacket pocket for the box cutter he'd lifted from the loading area behind a liquor store.

He opened the box cutter and knelt down to start the grisly work. The moment the blade touched Castillo's throat, the fat man's rapidly swelling eyes opened. Castillo grabbed hold of him and – with what Granger figured must be adrenalin-fueled strength – hurled him into the cabinets beneath the counter. The box cutter clattered to the floor.

Castillo was on his knees quickly and crawling toward Granger with a murderous look in his eyes.

Granger reached above his head and onto the counter, feeling around for the filet knife that Castillo had tried to grab earlier. His fingers found the knife just as Castillo reached him, almost smothering him with his mass. Granger gripped the plastic handle tight.

"I'll kill you," Castillo mumbled through broken teeth and a bloodied mouth.

Granger brought the knife down at an angle, slashing across Castillo's eye, across the bridge of his nose and into his cheek. Castillo howled.

Flipping his wrist, Granger changed the direction of the blade and slashed across Castillo's throat, opening it wide. Hot blood splashed across Granger's face and chest and Castillo fell, bleeding and gurgling, on top of Granger.

It took all of his strength to push the fat man off him. Blood coated Granger, sticky and cooling rapidly on his skin, and he wasn't at all happy about it.

He grabbed the box cutter, stood slowly and looked down at Castillo's corpse, a bag of meat and bone. Maybe he was losing his touch. It hadn't gone as smoothly as he had hoped, but it was done. And that was money in the bank, quite literally.

Then, the girl upstairs that he had all but forgotten about started screaming.

Even though common sense and instinct told him that is was time to get the hell out of Dodge, he couldn't leave the girl. He hurried through the living room, which was just as messy and cluttered as the kitchen, with more pizza boxes and fast food containers strewn about on the floor.

The television was on a news station, and as he made his way to the stairs Granger could hear the deep, practiced voice of a newscaster. Something was happening at the airport. Maybe they grounded planes because of the snow. That would make leaving town even more difficult. The night just kept getting better and better.

He reached the top of the stairs and it smelled just as noxious and rotten as the rest of the house. The girl kept screaming, making it easier to find her but increasing the chance that the neighbors were going to call the cops.

Granger opened the door leading to the screams and turned on the light. The room was plastered with porn, torn from magazines and taped to the wall to create a jumble of twisted, flesh-colored wallpaper.

He found the girl tied to a bed with rope. She was staring at Granger, a look of anger and fear in her eyes.

Granger realized he must look like a wreck, all covered in blood. Way to go, hero. "I'm not gonna hurt you. I'm here to help."

The girl was Asian, and no more than fourteen or fifteen, nothing but a baby. She wore jeans, a Jesus Saves t-shirt and pink boots.

She was just a little thing.

"He can't hurt you anymore," Granger said. "I'm gonna get you out of here, okay?"

Castillo was a real sick fuck; there was no doubt about that. Granger wish he'd had more time to spend making him suffer. He used the box cutter to slice through the ropes that bound her hands and feet to the four-poster bed. When she was free she stood, but she looked wobbly.

"Haven't stood in a while," she said, leaning against one of the bedposts, keeping here eyes on him. "How did you find me? Are you a cop?"

He couldn't very well tell her the truth, so he avoided the subject completely. "I'm gonna take you to a hospital, okay. They will be able to help you."

"Are you an angel?"

Granger almost laughed. People had called him many things in his life, but *angel* was never one of them. "You okay to walk now?"

She nodded. "Did you kill him?"

Granger said nothing. He found her coat, wrapped it around her shoulders, and together headed downstairs. He wanted to avoid the kitchen so she didn't have to see the mess even though that meant that they would have to leave by the front door.

When they got to the base of the stairs, Granger heard something in the kitchen. It sounded as though someone were *eating*. No way could Castillo still be alive. And even if he were, why the hell would he be eating something after getting his throat cut? It had to be an animal or something. Maybe the rats he'd seen scurry from the kitchen before had come back and started working on Castillo en masse. Still, he had to check, make sure that Castillo was dead.

He looked down at the girl and whispered, "Wait here."

"Don't leave me," she said, her eyes pleading with him.

"I don't want you to go through the kitchen," he said.

She gripped his arm. "Don't leave me. If he's dead, I want to see. I need to see."

Granger was no psychologist, but maybe she *should* see the body of the man that kidnapped her. That way she would know that he would never threaten her again. He knew that if her were in her position that's just what he would've wanted.

"Okay," he said. He opened the box cutter again and held it in his free hand. The girl was clinging to his other.

He pushed open the swinging door that led to the kitchen and peered inside. He could feel the girl peeking around him to see.

Castillo was still on the floor in a pool of his own blood, but he was not alone. The man that Granger had seen earlier, the one that had gotten out of his SUV and vomited all over himself, was now in the kitchen, hunkered down over Castillo's body. He was chewing on Castillo's face.

A boy not more than ten years old stood behind the feasting man, watching with glistening pure black eyes. He had a large hole in the side of his neck that oozed something black and viscous. The boy wasn't just watching, Granger thought. He's waiting his turn.

The girl's grip tightened on his arm, and she whispered. "They're demons."

The man looked up at the sound, a bit of Castillo's nose hanging from his lips. He sniffed the air and then his eyes, pitch black eyes, settled on the door where they stood.

The man rose from the floor and tried to say something, but it came out as a wheeze. The boy started forward, lurching toward them.

On the filthy linoleum floor, Granger saw Castillo move.

## 5.

Sirens blared outside, and Preacher could hear people shouting. Gunshots rang out in the distance. He forgot about the sandwich he still held in his hand.

He looked over at Junebug, who was watching the shadows of the warehouse. The fire didn't give off much light, so there were plenty of shadows to watch.

"What's all that about?" Preacher said.

"I don't know. Maybe it has something to do with those people coming out of O'Hare. They said there were riots or something," Junebug said.

"Nah," Preacher said. "We aren't even close to the airport."

"What do you think then?" Junebug said, turning to face Preacher. "Sounds like a fucking warzone out there."

Junebug was right. It did sound like war, at least what Preacher imagined a war might sound like.

Something bad was happening, and it was happening right outside. That much was certain.

The shouts turned into screams and the gunshots slowly died out. Curiosity finally got the better of Preacher.

"I'm gonna go take a look," he said.

"Are you crazy or stupid?" Junebug said. "You don't want any of what's going on out there. Shit, we don't even know what's happening. Use your head, my man, so you don't get it shot off your fool neck."

Preacher shook his head. He wouldn't be able to get back to his sandwich in peace unless he knew what was happening. He didn't make it to the edge of the firelight before he heard something coming toward him. He could hear what sounded like footsteps shuffling through the blackness.

"Hello," he said. "Who's that?"

The sound grew closer. Fear knotted Preacher's stomach. Something wasn't right about this. Cops would have announced themselves; anybody they knew on the street would have done the same, even if it were that asshole, Cole, come to steal their spot again. This had something to do with what was happening outside, he was sure of it.

"Cole, is that you?" Junebug asked as he joined Preacher. The shadows of the vast warehouse made it impossible to see much of anything.

"Creepy, ain't it?" Junebug said.

"Damn straight," said Preacher. He was about to say that maybe they should leave and find somewhere else to hole up when he heard it.

A low, creaking sound emanated from the darkness. It sounded as though someone were groaning but couldn't quite get the breath to do it properly.

158

"What the fuck is that?" Junebug said.

Another one of the groans joined the first, and then another and another, until there was a near deafening chorus.

"Let's get out of here. Now," Preacher said. He didn't want to play with whoever was trying to scare them off. It wasn't worth the trouble, not worth fighting over and ending up dead on Christmas Eve.

"We're leaving," Junebug called into the darkness. "Hope you're happy . . . assholes."

The groaning grew louder and the footsteps came closer. Preacher could see shapes in the darkness now. He shot Junebug a glare. Junebug just couldn't keep his mouth shut, had to go and make trouble slide from bad to worse.

They quickened their pace, heading to the rear of the warehouse and away from the fire barrel. They could slip through the back and be outside where it was colder but there would be fewer nutcases.

The groans suddenly stopped. The sound of the footsteps intensified. More people, Preacher thought. What did they want?

"We said we're leaving," Preacher said, screwing up his courage. He didn't want confrontation; he just wanted to leave. "Just let us on out of here."

"Hungry," one of the creaking voices called in the dark. The voice didn't sound at all human. "So *hungreeeeee!*"

Preacher looked over his shoulder and he could see them in the firelight now. They were people he knew, yet they weren't right. Their faces were different, torn and ripped. Many of them had patches of skin missing from their necks and their faces, and their eyes were

159

hollow. But the light was poor, and Preacher persuaded himself that it had to be just a trick of the light.

Cole Jones was at the center of a group of torn up homeless. He was a big man with nasty dreadlocks and a perpetual grimace. Part of his neck had a hole in it, on his dirty gray sweatshirt it looked like there were bullet holes. Preacher had always thought Cole was intimidating, the street equivalent of a high school bully. Now he made Preacher's skin crawl even more.

Preacher could see others with them, and it wasn't just the people of the street. He saw two uniformed cops, Randers and Deal. Those two were good guys, never gave him any shit and fed him on more than on occasion. A girl named Angie, who worked down at the gas station over on Fullerton Avenue, was with them. They weren't the same now. They all had that hollow stare. What had happened to them?

"Holy, jumpin' H. Christ," Junebug said. "Something fucked them up royally."

"Run," Preacher whispered. Trick of the light or not, he didn't want to be there anymore.

He and Junebug took off running toward the back door. Preacher hoped that it hadn't already snowed enough to block the door and hold it shut.

# 6.

Holly ran from the diner as fast as her feet would carry her, slipping once in the ankle deep the snow and nearly falling before she finally reached her car.

It was then that two things struck her. First, it was unbelievably cold. Second, she didn't have her keys. Along with her cell phone, the keys sat safely tucked away in the pocket of her nice warm jacket that was hanging in the back room of the Fry Shack.

*Son of a bitch.*

No way was she going to go back into the diner after her keys, not after what she'd seen. That *thing* had been chewing on Mitch, eating him. She'd rather freeze than go back in there.

Her car was the only one in the diner parking lot. Mitch had always taken the bus to and from work or bummed a ride from her.

Poor Mitch.

His screams had stopped, but Holly could hear them still echoing in her mind. Mitch's son was at home and waiting alone for his father who would never return. At least it hadn't been her though. As selfish as the thought was, she wasn't sorry for having it. Mitch shouldn't have gotten so close to the freak . . . the freak that was still in there chewing on him.

Where the fuck was a cop when you needed one? If she had wanted to buy some weed, you could be damn sure there would be cops lurking around.

A traffic light at the end of the road blinked red through the steadily falling snow. The streets were empty, everyone gone home early. Mitch was even going to close the diner early so they could get home. He still had to wrap presents.

As she was contemplating the best direction to walk to find help, she heard a familiar sound: the tinkling of the bell on the diner's door as it opened. Flannel Man came out covered in Mitch's blood, dripping crimson onto the walkway. Her heart nearly stopped, and she suddenly didn't feel the cold anymore, just fear. She ducked behind her car quick as she could and dropped to the ground to lay flat on the snow.

Peering through the gap between the bottom of her car and the ground, she could see Flannel Man trudging slowly through the snow. He stopped for a moment and she thought she could hear him sniffing the air. Then he started moving again, walking across the parking lot. He wasn't heading in her direction though. He was walking toward the street. She watched until she couldn't see him anymore and then slowly pushed herself to her knees and looked over the hood of her car.

Flannel Man continued to walk, not looking back. He seemed to be moving faster now, or at least without the slow and jerky movements she'd seen in the diner.

As Holly watched him go, she thought she could see other people farther down the street; at least half a dozen and they were heading right for Flannel Man. She wondered if she should call out and warn them. He might come back if she did. *Keys first*, she thought. Keys were the most important thing. Get the keys, quick and quiet. Then she could get help and there would be no more Flannel Man, no more cannibalistic weirdo.

Holly hurried back to the diner and stopped at the door. God, she didn't want to have to see Mitch's body. She took a deep breath and jerked open the door. The sound of the bells on the door set her heart to racing. Could Flannel Man hear them? Would he be back? No time to care.

She stepped into the diner and couldn't help but look at Mitch just the way that she always looked at accidents on the freeway. He lay on the floor, shirt covered in blood, parts of his face and neck gnawed to the bone. He was missing hunks of flesh from his shoulder and chest as well.

She heaved and thought she might throw up then turned quickly away and hurried through to the break room. It was a small room painted a pastel yellow and it held only a tattered loveseat, a radio, and the perpetual smell of fried food.

She grabbed her jacket, which was next to Mitch's trench coat, and reached into the pocket. Her keys and phone were there just as they should be.

She turned the phone on and dialed 911 but couldn't get through. Panic started to set in again and then she remembered the manager's office. It had a landline. She might be able to get through to the police on that phone, as long as Mitch hadn't already locked the door leading to the office. She tried the knob, but it didn't turn. That meant Mitch had the keys in his pocket. No fucking way was she going to go after the office keys. She would just get away, drive to a cop shop and be done with it.

When she reached the front of the diner, Mitch was waiting for her. His eyes were now black, just like those of Flannel Man. He sniffed the air and then seemed to taste it with his now black tongue.

"My Holly," he said. The words were nothing more than whispered groans. "Take me home, Holly."

Her mind froze for a fraction of a second, trying to register everything that was happening. Then she realized that she didn't care what was happening. She just needed to get out, get to her car. Just because Mitch was dead and then *wasn't* dead anymore didn't change anything. Yeah, right. The walking dead didn't change anything.

Holly had a straight shot for the door and she took it. She burst out through the doors in fear of her life and sanity for the second time in less than ten minutes.

Her foot hit a slippery patch of snow and fell on her ass. She barely felt the pain and she was able to keep hold on the keys. Her phone skittered away, buried in the snow.

Behind her, she could hear the bells on the door when it opened. Mitch was coming. She scrambled back to her feet, started toward her car and stopped just as suddenly.

Flannel Man and the six others she'd seen walking down the road toward him were waiting at her car, sniffing the air. They were just as dead as he was. Flannel Man hadn't gone to attack them; he'd gone to *get* them. Somehow, they reminded her of a pack of feral dogs like the ones that hung around down by the park. They were hungry and they were hunting. They were hunting her. They started forward when they saw her, moving with more speed than she'd seen when they were coming down the road.

Mitch's voice groaned from just behind her. "Take me home, Holly." She turned away from the car, away from the diner, and ran blindly into the night.

Holly kept running, not daring to turn around. She knew they were still back there, not as fast as she was, but they were gaining. The cold didn't seem to bother them at all.

The streets were empty. No people in this area; there were only closed businesses with signs in the window that said they would be back after the holiday. She put her head down, kept running despite the cramps in her legs, and the burning in her chest. She turned a corner and ran straight into a man who grabbed at her, and they both tumbled to the ground.

## 7.

Granger backed away from the door. He couldn't have seen Castillo move; that was impossible. The guy was dead, no doubt about that. Yet Granger knew enough to trust his eyes. Castillo *had* moved.

Keeping the girl behind him, eyes on the swinging kitchen door, Granger backed toward the front door.

The kitchen door started to swing in toward the living room. Granger could hear several deep groans coming from the kitchen. Granger couldn't tell if they were growling or wheezing.

"Let's get out of here," he said. He wished that he had something more substantial than a box cutter for defense, but it would have to do for now. As they left through the front door and stepped into the snowy night, Granger chanced to look over his shoulder. He didn't want one of the – *whatever they were* – to rush him.

Two of the things, the man and (presumably) his son, fought to get through the kitchen doorway, clambering over one another.

Granger could also see a third form standing behind them. It was Castillo, without a doubt, still in his bright red Santa jacket. Back from the dead, with his ruined face, slashed throat and all. Castillo sniffed the air and locked his black eyes with Granger.

"I thought he was dead," the girl said. Her grip on Granger's arm tightened.

"Yeah, me too," Granger said. "Come on."

They started to run down the block toward the car. Granger's legs were much longer than the girl's were. He stopped a moment, picked her up in one arm, and then continued running. She was light – couldn't weigh more than eighty pounds. Granger found himself wondering if Castillo had been starving her or if she were always that light; not that it mattered now.

When they reached the car, he set her on the ground so that he could open the front door. She climbed through the driver's side and into the passenger seat.

Granger looked back in the direction from which they'd come to see if Castillo was following. He was, and in addition to the father and son duo, three others had joined them. They were walking slowly down the street, fixed on the car. Their movements were unsteady, jerking and twitching, but they seemed to be getting better control of their ambulation with each step they took.

Granger could see Castillo's face, brow furrowed and lips twisted into a snarl. Through the falling snow and in the streetlamp's illumination, the cuts on his face and throat appeared black. Granger couldn't turn away, fascinated by the walking dead.

"Mister," the girl said, softly. "We have to get out of here."

Her soft voice brought him out of his daze. "Yeah," he said, getting into the car and starting the engine. "Yeah, we do."

As he pulled away from the curb and stepped on the gas, he looked in the rearview mirror. Castillo still walked onward, following. His image grew smaller as the car sped away.

They drove in silence for a moment.

"You saw what I saw, right?" Granger asked, questioning his own sanity. Maybe all the years of wetwork had finally gotten to him, made him snap.

That was more likely than a dead man getting up and chasing him was.

"I saw them," she said. "Demons, I think. You aren't crazy."

"I don't believe in demons. At least not demons like that," Granger said. Hell, he didn't believe in much, not unless it involved a payday. The only *demons* he knew were the ones that people pushed away and hid, things best left buried.

"What do you think they were then?" she asked.

"Hell if I know," he said. The streets were mostly devoid of people, but he saw a few walking through the snow here and there. Some of them were in their nightclothes, bites visible along their throats and on their arms. He wanted to get out of the neighborhood, out of Chicago, and back to Cali where things made sense. "I don't know."

"Faith," she said.

"I don't really have any," Granger replied.

"No, *I'm* Faith. That's my name, mister. I'm Faith Baltazar." She seemed amused, which Granger thought was strange, given their situation. She hadn't cried and she barely seemed scared except for those first few minutes when he had found her upstairs.

"Oh," he said, glancing at her Jesus Saves shirt. "That makes sense."

"What's your name? I don't wanna have to keep calling you mister."

"It's," he began and then thought better of it. Why give this girl his name? He was just going to dump her at the nearest hospital. She didn't need his name. With his name, the police would be able to find him and charge him with Castillo's murder. Then again, Castillo wasn't exactly dead now was he? What exactly was

Castillo . . . what were those other things with him, eating him?

"I'm waiting," Faith said.

"I'm Granger," he said.

He turned a corner, heading past the liquor store where he'd taken the box cutter less than a quarter mile from Castillo's house. The store wasn't open, but he could see a few people wandering around in the parking lot. Why would they –

"They're like the others back at his house," she said.

"You think so?" He slowed down a bit to get a better look. When the car slowed, their heads snapped up, focused on the vehicle. Then they started moving toward the car. She was right; they were the same.

"Damn," he said. He gunned the engine and took off. More of the things were coming out of the side streets and alleys now. "What's going on here?"

"I think it's the end," Faith said. "You know, the dead walking the earth and all."

"Is that Bible prophecy or something?"

"Something," she said.

"I'm not really a believer in all that," Granger said. "It's gotta be some kind of contagion. Yeah, it'll turn out to be something like that, you'll see. The CDC will get up here and take care of it before it gets out of hand."

"The CDC?" she said.

"It's the Center for Disease Control. They take care of things like this."

Gunshots and sirens sounded in the distance. It wasn't sounding like a very good night for anyone.

"I'm fifteen, not stupid. I know what the CDC is. What I mean is *how* are they going to take care of it?

Things like this don't happen," Faith said. "They aren't going to know what to do."

Once again, he knew she was right. Granger didn't believe the CDC could handle whatever was happening any more than Faith did. He'd just wanted to give her some measure of comfort. She'd been through a hell of a lot already. Maybe he was trying to comfort himself too.

"Well, the first thing we do is find some people, people that aren't affected or *infected* by what's happening," Granger said. Dumping her at a hospital was out though. If more people had this . . . whatever it was, then the hospital would be the last place he wanted to go. "Then we'll go from there."

He slowed the car a bit. The snow was coming down fast and the roads were getting slick. Through the falling snow, he could see silhouettes of people on the sidewalks and in parking lot. How long before the city was gone?

Faith turned on the radio. The station was still playing Christmas songs. *God Rest Ye Merry, Gentlemen* poured from the speakers.

Granger wondered why they were still playing the Christmas songs and why there wasn't a news broadcast about what was happening. Then he figured the people at the station must have simply programmed the songs to play while no one was there over the holidays.

"I like this one," Faith said. "My family sings it on Christmas."

"Where is your family? What part of Chicago are they in? Maybe we should go there so they know you're okay. They've gotta be worried."

"They don't live in Chicago," she said. "They're still in the Philippines. They sent me here so I'd be less trouble I guess. I was going to school at Lake Forest Academy when that man took me."

"How long . . . how long were you there at his house?"

"Two days. He plays Santa at Atrium Mall. He followed me and grabbed me when I was on the way to the bus stop."

"You're too young to be riding the bus in this town . . . or any other town for that matter. It's dangerous," Granger said, feeling suddenly paternal even though he'd never even given a thought to having children of his own. The only thing he'd ever been able to "raise" successfully was a ball python named Mal.

"You're about three days too late for that lecture," she said. "And he hadn't . . . he hadn't done anything to me yet. He said I was going to be his Christmas gift. He said that he'd been a good boy all year and that tomorrow he would open me."

She said it as though it were a normal part of conversation. She was either the toughest person he'd ever met – and he'd met some tough SOBs – or the best actress in the world. Or maybe it just hadn't all sunk in yet.

"Castillo was a sick fuck," he said. He quickly added, "Sorry about the language."

"I've heard worse than that," Faith said. "Castillo was his name, huh?"

"Yeah," Granger said.

"I think he still wants me. I think that's what he was doing when he was sniffing. I think he's going to follow us like an animal or something."

170

"I don't think that's possible. Senses aren't that good, not with people anyway," Granger said. "Besides, I think we're too far away now."

"You don't think he or any of these other things are still human do you?" Faith asked. "He's going to find me."

"Well if he does, I'll just have to kill him again, won't I?" Granger said.

"Cut his head off," Faith said, still flipping through the radio stations. "If he comes back, you should cut his head off."

"Yeah, that should do it," Granger said. "That'll be a hell of a job with my box cutter though."

Faith changed to the AM stations and finally found one that had an actual broadcast though the static made it difficult to hear everything. According to the broadcaster on the radio, there was no need to panic. It was simply rioting. That was bullshit and Granger was sure everyone who had seen one of those things would agree. Of course, the broadcast didn't give a reason for the outbreak of the so-called riots; they only said that people should stay inside and let the authorities handle things. They mentioned something about the National Guard and then there was more static.

If it were just contained to a few areas in Chicago, they might be safe if they just left the city. Granger opened his mouth to ask Faith if she knew the best way to get out of the city when a dark form lurched off the sidewalk and toward the car.

He barely saw it through the falling snow. He jerked the steering wheel and the car began to slide out of control. The driver's side smashed into the once human creature, knocking it flat. The car careened, spinning on the snow until the front end crashed into city bus parked on the side of the street. The crash wasn't bad, but it jerked him forward. The airbags never deployed, and he made a mental note never to rent from that car agency again. Not that it was likely he would have the chance to worry about it.

"Are you okay?" Faith asked, rubbing her shoulder.

"Shaken and stirred," he said. He looked out the window and he could see several shapes coming through the snow toward the car. "Oh, shit. We gotta get out of here. Now."

# 8.

The impact sent Preacher to the ground hard and fast. The iron pipe he had in his hand clattered to the ground. A pain shot through the muscles of his back when he landed on the snow covered alley. The woman was on top of him, and the only thing Preacher could imagine was her teeth sinking into him and staring into her dark eyes, black eyes like Cole and all of those other monsters now had.

He fought to push her off him. She was light, but she was fighting him. Strangely, she was not trying to bite as he'd seen those other monstrosities doing to people since he and Junebug fled the warehouse. No, she was fighting with her hands and she was screaming.

Junebug grabbed the woman around the waist and hauled her up.

"Stop it," he said. He was trying to get her flailing arms under control. "Stop it unless you want them to hear you, moron."

Preacher sat up, his back rife with a hot searing pain. The woman had stopped struggling and

172

screaming but it looked like she was crying now. Beneath her coat, she wore what looked like a waitress's uniform and she was shivering. She wasn't one of the monsters.

He struggled to his feet. His old body didn't respond well to all this running. Crashing into the woman certainly hadn't helped matters.

"Hush now," Junebug said, still trying to calm the woman. "We ain't gonna hurt you."

"They're coming," she said, once again trying to break free of the grasp Junebug had on her. "They were right behind me."

"Well then we're in a hell of a pickle," Junebug said. "We got some of those fuckers on our tail too."

"Stick with us," Preacher said, extending a hand to her. "We can find someplace to hole up until all this is over."

The woman nodded, but she didn't take Preacher's hand. "I'm Holly."

"I'm Preacher," he said, withdrawing his hand. "This is Junebug."

"Pleased to meet you," Junebug said, letting her go. "Let's do introductions and all those niceties later. In case you forgot, the fucking world is coming to an end."

"Where can we go?" Holly asked.

Preacher didn't know what to tell her. Where *could* they go? The things were overrunning the streets. The open buildings and warehouses and abandoned houses were no good either. He didn't know what to tell her. "Somewhere safer than here."

The trio hurried down the alley the way Junebug and Preacher had come. Preacher listened for sounds of pursuit as best he could. He couldn't tell if the things, the monsters as he'd come to call them, were nearby or not. It was hard to hear anything with sirens, the occasional gunshot ringing out, and, once, what sounded like a car crash from somewhere ahead of them. The city was a warzone. Thankfully, they weren't in a heavy residential area. He couldn't imagine what kind of hell it would be like in an area with more people. It was mostly some homeless out here and some people caught out on the streets. As well as a few idiots who didn't have the sense to stay hidden.

They'd nearly gotten to the end of the street without seeing anymore of the monsters. The burning pain in Preacher's back continued.

That was when they heard them, the guttural, inhuman moans coming from the street ahead. The damned things were everywhere, growing in number. Preacher didn't think it sounded as though the monsters were moving toward the alley. They sounded like they were fixated on something else.

Preacher knew how they did it too, how they came back. He didn't know the mechanics of it, but he'd seen it in action not more than half an hour earlier.

He and Junebug had escaped Cole and the creatures in the warehouse and then laid low as best they could. They watched as Cole and several of the creatures traveling with him tore apart an old man and woman not far from the warehouse. Preacher had wanted to shout to them, to warn them, but Junebug clamped a hand over his mouth and told him that doing that would just get them killed too.

So, unable to turn his gaze away, he watched. The elderly couple went down quickly. Preacher heard the creatures' teeth gnashing and tearing into them. It wasn't but a couple of minutes later when the old man and his old lady stood up, monsters themselves now. Whatever it was, some kind of sickness or something, it worked damn quickly. Preacher didn't want any part of that. Despite his last name, he wasn't a God fearing individual. Well, he hadn't been, not until tonight.

He shook from his head the thought of the old man and woman rising after the monsters murdered them. He knew he needed to be alert, needed to keep his ears open. He strained again to hear.

In addition to the moans, he heard a scream and a shout. The scream sounded an awful lot like a child. The old folks were one thing; they'd had a chance to live their lives. Not a kid though; he couldn't handle that. He started forward, toward the direction of the scream, his pain not forgotten but pushed down with adrenalin.

He felt Junebug put a hand on his shoulder. "What the fuck you think you're doing?"

"I can't let some kid get bit by one of them things," Preacher said, shrugging off Junebug's hand.

"You're crazy," Holly said. "Let's just go. They're already dead."

"You don't know that," Preacher said. "I can't just stand by." Preacher turned away and began walking toward the moans. The child's shriek echoed through the night once more and he quickened his pace.

"Damn it all," Junebug said. "You ain't going without me."

Preacher heard Junebug's heavy footfalls in the snow behind him, hurrying to catch up. The waitress, Holly, didn't seem pleased.

"You've got to be fucking kidding me," she said. She didn't move. "You said we'd find somewhere safe."

Preacher kept going, gripping the frigid iron pipe tight in his hand.

## 9.

Holly peered around the corner. She could see six of the creatures closing in on the car, with more in the distance and coming closer every second. One of the creatures coming up the block and leading a gang of others was dressed as Santa Claus, except that he wasn't wearing any pants. It would have made her laugh if not for the fear.

She watched Junebug and Preacher rushing through the snow, a pipe raised above Preacher's head. Those idiots were going to get themselves killed, and she would be alone again. The assholes shouldn't have left her.

Holly watched as a man climbed out of the car. He was tall and he was good looking. He also looked very pissed. He reached into the car and helped another person out, a young girl by the looks of it. Was it his daughter? No, she looked Asian and the man was very definitely white. Maybe he'd adopted her or a she was a stepdaughter.

She shook her head slightly. It was the end of the world and she was trying to figure out the guy's situation. Definitely not one of the smartest things to do.

"Hey," she heard Preacher yell at the creature (for she was sure they weren't human, not anymore) closest to him.

The thing turned its head just in time to catch an iron pipe to the skull. The impact, a dull wet thud, dropped the creature to its knees. It opened its mouth and Preacher smashed it again, breaking the skull and spilling the thing's brains onto the fresh snow. Holly had never seen human brains, but she was sure they wouldn't look like this, all black and pulsing.

The other creatures turned their attention to their fallen comrade. They stared at the fallen and then turned, eyes fixed upon Preacher.

"Come on!" Preacher roared.

Holly didn't think the guy had that much fight in him. He was scary, standing there and swinging his iron pipe like a sword, smashing the jaw of one advancing creature and then the crown of the skull on another.

Junebug tried to draw the attention of the other three creatures. It didn't seem as though he or Preacher even noticed the others that were now nearing the car. The man did though. He shouted something that Holly couldn't hear amid the chaos.

Preacher and Junebug started to back away from the car, the man and girl coming with them, rushing now. They'd seen Santa Claus and his not-so-merry band of dead elves.

"Come on," Holly shouted, "Hurry." Santa and the others were getting closer.

The tiny hairs on the back of her neck suddenly stood up. In front of her, Preacher stopped and stared – no, *behind* her. His eyes were wide.

"Holly," Mitch said. His voice was barely a whisper, forced and dry. "Take me home, Holly."

177

## 10.

Granger didn't have time to thank the men that had helped him and Faith escape the monsters. As the four of them started toward the alleyway, Granger saw their companion, a woman. One of the dead things was about to take a bite out of her. Its mouth opened wide and the woman screamed. Granger could see her trying to get away, but the thing had a hold of her coat.

As the thing's mouth started to descend, a snowball hit it between the eyes. It stepped back, loosing its grip on the woman's coat. She took advantage of the opportunity to run towards the men that had just helped him and Faith.

A second snowball smacked the thing in the head. Granger turned to see Faith scooping up a handful of snow, quickly shaping it into a ball. The kid had a hell of an arm, but throwing snowballs at the monstrosities wouldn't do much good.

"Let's go," he said, grabbing Faith's hand as she launched a third snowball and hit the apron-wearing thing in its exposed throat.

They ran, following the woman and their saviors down the street toward who knew what other dangers. After a few blocks, they stopped to catch their breath.

Most of the buildings in the area were businesses and offices. Granger noted that there seemed to be fewer of the dead things here. He wondered how many of the dead were wandering around the city now. Except for the ones he was now with, he hadn't seen any living people on the streets.

He looked behind him and could see the creatures walking steadily toward them, not running – he didn't

178

think the things were able to run. It was as if their motor skills had diminished after they died and came back. Maybe they were like toddlers now; maybe they would learn how to run at some point in their *un*-life.

Castillo was there, leading the pack. The red of the Santa coat was easily visible. How had he caught up to them so quickly? Granger didn't know his way around Chicago, but he couldn't imagine that Castillo would be able to come that far that quickly. Had he gotten that turned around when the dead man came back to life and he fled the house with Faith? They had to be more than a mile away from that house by now. Some professional he was.

"Name's Preacher," said the black man that had smashed the hell out of three of the creatures. He extended his hand and Granger took it. "This is Junebug, and that's Holly."

"Thank you. I'm Granger," he said. "This is Faith. You saved our skin."

"Once again with the fucking introductions! Seriously, Preach, wait until we get somewhere safer than the middle of the street with thirty of those fucking things chasing us," the Junebug said. "They ain't but two blocks back, and who knows what else is around us. We're sitting out here like prime rib in the meat city."

He had a point. The woman who had nearly had her throat torn out was sobbing, near hysterical. Granger couldn't blame her. He'd been close to death plenty of times, but nothing like this. Faith shivered next to him, and he wondered how she was doing. Holding up better than the hysterical woman was that was sure.

"Where is safe?" Granger asked. "Warm too."

Preacher shrugged. "I haven't thought that far ahead yet."

"Walk and talk, people," Junebug said. He put a hand on the woman's shoulders. "Come on now, stop that bawling. They gonna hear you all the way down at Navy Pier."

They walked at a brisk pace, Granger scanning the side streets and turning to look behind him every ten steps. They were still back there, stalking slowly forward. The snow, coming down even harder, obscured them somewhat. He could see them though, dozens of dark shapes on the hunt.

He thought back to stories his uncle used to tell him about hunting. One of the techniques his uncle explained was driving the prey. Several hunters would walk through the woods, not caring if they were seen or if they made any sound. Their walking through the woods would send the deer hurrying away from them, directly to the other side of the woods where other hunters were already waiting. As soon as the animals came into range, the hunters would shoot them down.

Was that what those things were doing now? Were they that intelligent? They couldn't be organized enough to do that. They were dead, as much as that tore at the reality he thought he knew. They couldn't be able to communicate. What if they were; what if they were driving Granger and the others into a trap? Maybe that was why they were so nonchalant in the hunt.

"Hey," Granger said. "I don't trust this. It's like . . ."

"It's like we're being herded toward something," Preacher said. "I got that feeling too."

"Someplace safe," the woman mumbled. "That's what you promised."

180

"We need to get inside somewhere," Granger said. "Someplace dry, someplace warmer than out here. We can get our bearings and figure out what to do from there. We can't let those things push us into a trap."

"What do you suggest?" Junebug asked. "Where *can't* those things go?"

He scanned the streets again. More businesses and a small office park off to the left. They might be able to get into a building . . . that could work. At least for a little while, at least long enough to warm up and come up with a better idea.

Of course, there was always the possibility that they would simply be walking into a trap of their own design.

## 11.

It wasn't the best idea, but it was better than freezing. Preacher just didn't know if it was smart to stay in one place. The things would know where they were and they would gather outside the building. There wouldn't be any way to get out if the monsters found a way to get into the building. Not that he would've been able to go much farther with his jacked up back anyway. It felt like it was on fire.

They had found a two-story office building, Kramer's Paper Supply, which looked suitable. It was in an office park and had a small, attached warehouse. The only vehicles in the parking lot were three large white vans with the company logo on the side.

The building had three entrances, every one of them locked. Granger had used Preacher's iron pipe to smash through the lower portion of the glass door at the main entrance. It took some doing and made a lot of racket, and Preacher kept glancing over his shoulder expecting to see an army of the monsters marching up behind him.

Preacher figured there would be alarms in the building, but he didn't hear anything at all when the glass broke. That was good. It would have been like a dinner bell to the monsters. Granger told him it was probably a silent alarm alerting a security company, which would then phone the police. Not that the police would be here anytime soon, not with everything that was going down.

After getting inside, they took every damn thing imaginable, copiers, a desk, and more, to cover the hole at the main entrance and prevent the monsters from having easy access. The way everything was wedged against the door, Preacher didn't figure the things would be able to get in, at least not without making a lot of sound.

They had barricaded the other doors as well, which effectively trapped them in the building. Still, it was better than being outside with the monsters.

After securing everything, they retreated to the second floor, which held some offices, a long room of cubicles and a break room. The break room had vending machines, a refrigerator stocked with food, and a television. It even had a sofa, on which Preacher sat, his back about to give out. They might be able to stay here for a while as long as the monsters didn't get inside.

Granger turned on the television to one of the news channels, but it didn't tell them much. It was full of contradictions. No one seemed to have anything substantial in the way of information about the creatures other than that people should stay the hell away from them. They said the National Guard was securing the perimeter of the city and that they would then be sending troops in to quell the situation.

None of what they said made much sense. Each successive guest they had on contradicted the last until it devolved into petty arguing. They showed maps on screen of the infected areas, which was most of Chicago. Whatever was happening was affecting other cities too, Los Angles, London, Mexico City. Chicago seemed to be getting the worst of things though. They also showed a map of National Guard safe zones where people could be evacuated and quarantined. In the next breath, the news correspondent told everyone not to venture outside, that it wasn't safe.

"Load of crap", Preacher had mumbled to the television. He didn't know how people were supposed to get to the safe zones if they weren't supposed to leave the house though. Granger turned the volume down so they didn't have to listen. The television glow provided some light.

Preacher sank deeper into the sofa. It felt good, soft. He hadn't sat on anything that soft in a long time. Holly sat next to him, her eyes wide and vacant. She twitched at every sound, when the hands moved on the clock, when the icemaker in the refrigerator rattled. The poor woman was probably in shock, he thought. She would've been dead if it hadn't been for that little girl's amazing snowball arm. Holly hadn't even thanked the girl. But then, who was he to know what was going on in Holly's mind. The world had changed in the span of the past few hours. Who was he to judge?

"I don't have any money for the machines," said Faith.

"I'll fix that for you kiddo," Junebug said, snatching the still bloodied pipe that lay across Preacher's lap. Junebug quickly busted open the three vending machines and pulled out handfuls of candy. He tossed some chocolate bars at Preacher. "Eat up folks, eat it all."

"Thanks," Faith said, digging into the candy.

Granger stood at the window, looking outside.

"What you see out there?" Preacher asked. He wanted to get up and walk to the window himself, but his back wouldn't let him. He just needed to rest a few minutes and then he would be better. He hoped.

Granger kept his gaze focused on the outside. "They're gathering. I figured that would happen, but at least we're in here and they aren't."

"They'll find a way in," Holly said.

"I don't know if they're that smart," Junebug said. "I hope they ain't that smart. They'd have to do a lot of heavy lifting to get in here. I imagine those dead things would rather find some easier things to chew on than us."

"Not all of them," Faith said. "Some of them will leave, I think. But they aren't just *dead things* out there. They're demons, some of then want *us*."

Junebug laughed. "Sweetie, demons ain't real. If demons were real, then that would mean God were real. If God were real, do you think he'd let something like this happen to a kid like you?"

"What about you?" Faith said, turning toward Preacher. "You're a preacher. Don't you think they're demons?"

"Preacher's just my last name," he said. "It isn't my profession. I don't know what they are. You might even be right. They could be demons for all I know."

Junebug huffed. "You ask me, it's some kind of disease. Maybe it's something in the air."

"It's not in the air," Granger said, finally turning away from the window. "If it were the air, more people would have caught it. It's in their bite."

"Like a vampire then?" Faith asked. "That's almost like a demon, right?"

"They got it at the airport, I think," Holly said. "Or someone brought it here. The first one I saw, I called him Flannel Man, he had luggage with him. I think he'd just come from the airport."

Preacher sat up, back burning. "The airport makes sense." He nodded at Junebug. "You said something about O'Hare before all this started."

"Riots and whatnot," Junebug said. "People must've brought it with them on the plane. Maybe it's some kind of terrorist shit, Muslims or something."

"Maybe its Christians trying to usher in the Second Coming," Faith said, eyeing Junebug.

"Why would a good Christian do something like that?" Junebug asked. He ripped into another candy bar.

"Why would anyone do that? I think that was the point she was trying to make." Granger took a seat at one of the small round tables. "We don't know what happened and speculation probably isn't going to do us a lot of good. It hasn't done any good for all those people arguing on the news."

"If we knew for sure what they were, we might have a better idea of how to get away from them or stop them," Preacher said.

"You did a helluva job on their skulls with that pipe," Junebug said. "They didn't get up after that."

The memory of that sickened Preacher. Even though he was sure those bodies, the dead, were just shells it didn't make it any easier. He'd felt the skull give way, felt the breaking jaw, saw the blood and the strangely blackened brains. They'd been people once upon a time.

"There's too many to take on with a pipe," Granger said. "I think they're hunting us, and if they are that means they aren't mindless."

"Bah, you're crazy," Junebug said through a mouthful of chocolate. "They're dumb, just wandering around through the snow like that looking for some fools like us to be outside so they can have a quick snack."

"No, Granger's right," Holly said. "The man that almost killed me in that alley . . . I knew him. I worked with him and I saw him turn into one of them. His name was Mitch. The guy from the airport, Flannel Man, bit him."

"It didn't take long for the change, did it?" Preacher asked. He knew; he'd seen it happen too.

"Mitch changed in a few minutes," she said. "Flannel Man didn't look like he was bitten though."

"He was probably one of the original carriers, got it at the airport and it incubated. It might've just taken him slower," Granger said. "I saw a guy come home with a suitcase, went into his house. The change must have happened when he was inside with his family. He turned his son and they were waiting for us when we got downstairs."

"Why's it happen so fast now?" Holly asked. "It only took Mitch a few minutes to come back."

Granger shrugged. "Who knows? Maybe the people on the plane ingested something or breathed something in and it took longer. Maybe the disease, or whatever it is, travels faster through saliva and blood. Christ, maybe it is demons. Like I said earlier, it doesn't matter what it is. The end result is the same."

"What brought you here anyway," Junebug asked. "You aren't from Chicago; I can tell by the way you talk. If you was here to visit family for the holidays, you'd be worried about them right now, not sitting in here chatting with us."

"Work," Granger said. "Lucky me, I got Chicago on Christmas."

"Lucky you," Preacher said. Something about Granger seemed off. He moved like a man that knew how to take care of himself, he moved like a predator.

"He saved me from a very bad man, someone who was a bad man before all of this started," Faith said, seeming to sense Preacher's unease. "Granger's my angel."

Preacher looked into Faith's eyes now and he could see cracks in the little girl's brave façade. Something terrible had happened to her, something that went deeper than the roaming dead outside. He knew that haunted look. He might not know Granger enough to trust him, but if Faith had, well, *faith*, then that was good enough for him, at least for now.

"They move with a purpose," Granger said. He'd taken his post at the window again. "They are hunting us, I'm sure."

"Why you saying that?" Junebug asked. "I'm telling you, those things just wander around. I've seen movies about this shit. Z-O-M –"

"Because the *bad man* is there, and so is the one that tried to snack on Holly," Granger cut in before

Junebug could finish. This sent Holly into a fit of moans and whimpers beside Preacher.

Preacher stood and walked to the window, despite his back pain. He had to check, had to see how many of the things were out there. He also wanted to see if someone else had followed them, a face he didn't want to see again.

"If that's the case," Junebug said, "then you'd see a big ugly fellow with a whole mess of dreadlocks who has a massive hate on for me and Preacher."

Preacher got to the window and looked outside. At least fifty of the undead were there, and Cole Jones was staring up at the window and looking directly at Preacher. It sent a chill through his pained back.

Junebug joined him at the window and looked down into the mass of dead. "You know, this has to be one of the worst Christmases I've ever had."

"*One* of the worst?" Faith said from her seat at the table.

"Yeah," Junebug nodded. "I used to be married."

Preacher couldn't help but laugh.


# 12.

Holly knew they were going to kill her, knew they were going to use her to bait the dead so they could escape. Yes, they were selfish that way. She could tell. She would be a lure and the rest of them would be safe. She couldn't let that happen, couldn't let it. No, she needed to live. She was more important than they were, more important than some homeless pieces of garbage and some little Asian kid. What about Granger though? He seemed nice enough. He wouldn't do anything to her, wouldn't let them hurt her. Would he let them? Yes, he might. She didn't know him and no matter how attractive she thought he was, she could not trust him. She couldn't trust any of them, not if she wanted to live. She had to do something to protect herself and she had to do it soon.

A plan came to her then and it made perfect sense. Rather than letting them send her out into the mouths of the dead, she would bring the dead to them. She would give up her motley crew, let those monsters chew on their bones, and then she would be safe. That was what she had to do. After all, she didn't want to be late to her mother's Christmas party now did she?

"I have to go to the bathroom," Holly said, rising off the couch and stepping past Preacher's stinking body. She figured he probably smelled worse than the dead.

"You want one of us to go with you, make sure everything's safe?" Preacher asked.

Holly glanced down at him and grimaced. "I don't know you enough to have you hang out in the bathroom with me."

"Suit yourself. Be careful and holler if you need us," Junebug said.

She left the room quickly and navigated the dark hallway, trying to remember where the upstairs bathroom had been. She'd seen it when they came up the stairs somewhere down near the end of the hallway. Granger had said they couldn't turn on the lights when they came into the building because they didn't want to attract any more attention than they already had. They were all idiots. Every dead thing in a mile would be able to find them, to sniff them out just as Mitch had done. Light didn't make a shit's bit of difference.

It only took her a few minutes to locate the bathroom. She stepped inside and turned on the light. Holly didn't recognize the woman in the mirror. Her hair was askew, eye shadow dripping down her face so she looked like Alice Cooper. Caked blood covered her clothes and her face where Mitch had touched her. That wasn't Holly in the mirror. No, it was someone else. She was two people now and neither of them wanted to die.

She started to wash her face and then decided against it. There was no point. Instead, she turned off the light and went back to the dark hallway.

When she got downstairs, she could see the barricaded door through which they had come. They peered through the glass. Mitch was there, standing in front, hand pressed against the glass.

Poor Mitch. He didn't deserve this any more than she had. He wouldn't hurt her, not good old Mitch. He was her friend. She'd given him rides home. That was all he wanted, just a ride home. Maybe she could reason with him, let the dead come in and take Preacher and the others and she would take Mitch home. Yes, that seemed like a good idea. That would work. It might take her some time to remove the barricade, but she could do it.

She hurried toward the door, waving and smiling at Mitch. He neither waved nor smiled back. His mouth opened and closed though, and Holly knew what he was trying to say.

*Take me home, Holly.*

## 13.

Granger stared out the window. The crowd of dead thinned out until there were only a handful of them in the parking lot. Had they given up that easily? Granger doubted it. More likely than not they had seen some poor morsel outside and went to hunt. Or they were trying to find another way into the building.

While the Kramer building had given them some semblance of shelter and rest the past few hours, he didn't want to stay there. Eventually the dead would find their way into the building and then he and the others would have nowhere to run.

He looked at the trio of vans in the parking lot below. Driving would be better than walking as long as he didn't have another accident. He wasn't used to driving in the snow, but the van might provide better traction. He hoped. Now he just had to figure out where the keys might be and convince everyone else that it was a good idea to try to reach the vans.

Granger turned around from the window and saw Faith staring at him.

"Is he out there?" she asked.

Granger knew whom she meant. Castillo. He'd been there earlier, but he had moved off with the others. "Not anymore."

"You know he's just waiting. He still wants me," she said.

"I won't let that happen," said Granger. He'd never had to care for and watch over anyone, not like this. It was a strange feeling. Making sure that nothing happened to the child gave him more purpose than any of his contracts had ever done.

"I know you won't," she said. "I just wish I was dreaming or something."

"We all do, kid," Junebug said. The man was on his fifth or sixth candy bar – Granger had lost count, but he was sure Junebug must have been feeling one hell of a sugar rush.

Preacher hadn't spoken in some time and Granger knew the man was in agony from the pained look on his face any time he moved. Best to let him rest for a few more minutes. Holly was – *she was still in the bathroom*? She must have left at least fifteen minutes earlier. She should have been back by now.

"Faith, do you feel up to checking on Holly? I want her back here so I can to talk to everyone," Granger said.

Faith eyed the darkness beyond the break area for a moment and then nodded. "I can do that. We would have heard them if they had gotten in, right?"

"Yeah," Granger said. He was reasonably certain that they would have heard the things in the building. "If you don't want to go that's okay."

"I'll go," Junebug said.

"I'll be fine," Faith said. "Come find me if I scream though." Granger knew she was only half joking.

Granger turned his attention to Junebug. "I don't think we can stay here much longer. I think they're trying to find a way inside."

"I sure as shit don't wanna be trapped in here with those buggers," Junebug said. "You got a plan to get out without getting us all killed?"

"The vans," Granger said. "If we can find the keys to those vans, we might be able to drive to one of the safe zones on the outskirts of the city, the ones they were talking about on the news."

"I don't trust those," Junebug said. "But I suppose it beats sitting in here waiting to be a boxed lunch for those things."

"My thoughts exactly," Granger said.

"Where we gonna find the keys though?"

Preacher spoke up. He adjusted himself on the couch and Granger heard him wince through his words. "When I was a warehouse manager, people had to sign the vehicles out. We always kept the keys in my office on the upper floor. Smash and grab thieves weren't as likely to head upstairs, see, and even if someone knew where the keys were, having them upstairs would keep them in the building long enough that the cops could get there. At least that's how it worked in my building."

"You think we should take off too?" Junebug said.

"I don't think we have any other choice," said Preacher.

Junebug nodded. "I'll check the offices on this floor first, see what I can find. You guys figure out how to get to the van without us becoming a late night snack for those bastards."

Junebug wasn't gone five minutes before Faith started screaming.

## 14.

Holly grunted and pulled at the overturned copier machine. It was the last thing barricading the broken door. Some of the dead pushed on the copier from the outside. She thought she even saw Flannel Man in the throng. They were trying to help her. Mitch must've told them to help. Yes, she knew that was what must have happened. She would let them in for the others and then she would just take Mitch home. Afterwards, she could go home and get some rest. All she wanted to do was to put the night behind her. The morning would be brighter, yes it would.

She tugged harder on the copier, which snagged on the rubber mat just inside the door. Just a little bit more and she would be able to let them into the building.

"What are you doing?" asked a voice from behind her.

It was the child's small and grating voice. Maybe the others were sending her to do their dirty deeds. Holly would show them.

"What the fuck does it look like I'm doing?" Holly asked, grunting and moving the copier inch by inch. She peered over her shoulder and looked down the hallway at the girl's silhouette, barely visible. "I'm letting them inside."

"You're crazy," Faith said. She started to back away.

"Shut up," Holly said, turning back to her task. "They're going to eat you first," she said. "They told me so. They're going to do terrible things to you because you wanted to give me to them as bait."

One final heave and she managed to move the machine enough that they could start to crawl through the broken glass. Now it was almost over.

Mitch was the first one through, but that wasn't right. He was supposed to wait outside so Holly could take him home. That was the plan, right? That was what he wanted, just a ride home. Then why had he come into the building?

Clarity just started to set in as the chill from outside, along with the stink of the dead, hit her.

Mitch, mouth wide open, lunged forward and bit down on her neck.

The last thing Holly heard were the little girl's screams mingling with her own, and the last thing she thought about was how pissed offer her mother was going to be when she came home dead and bloody. Then there was blackness and silence as death washed over her.

## 15.

Preacher and Granger found Faith running up the stairwell to the second floor. Junebug was still looking for the keys, but Preacher knew he must have heard the kid's screams.

"What happened," Granger asked. "Are you okay?"

"She let them in," Faith said. She hurried up the stairs and together they went back into the hallway. Preacher closed the door behind them.

"What do you mean she let them in?" Granger asked, as they hurried down the hallway.

"Holly," Faith said. "It's like she just lost it. The man that tried to bite her before, the one I hit with the snowball, it was him that got her."

"Are you sure she's gone?" Preacher asked. He couldn't stomach the thought of leaving Holly alone down there with those things, not if there was something he could do.

"I'm sure," Faith said. Then, softly, "I'm very sure."

"Poor Holly," Preacher said. He'd only known her a few hours, but she shouldn't have had to go out like that.

"*Poor Holly* condemned the rest of us," Granger said.

"Her mind couldn't take it. I could feel her getting ready to snap. I should have said something," Preacher said. He knew Granger was right though. They *were* as good as condemned. Even if Junebug found the keys, there was no way they were going to be able to get to the doorway at the opposite end of the building and remove their barricades before the dead overran the place. With his back the way that it was, he wouldn't even be able to help move the barricade. They needed something to occupy the monsters.

Junebug darted out of one from the side offices and nearly scared Preacher to death.

"I got 'em! Found three sets of keys. Don't know which belongs to which van so I got 'em all. What was all that screaming about, everyone okay?"

"They got Holly," Preacher said. "She let them inside and they got her."

"Fuck. You mean they're in the building," Junebug whispered. "How we gonna get out now?"

"I don't know," Granger said. "We take the stairs at the opposite end of the building and try to remove the barricade before they know what we're doing."

"We ain't gonna be able to get that done in time. They'll be all over us," Junebug said. "The hallway downstairs is only a couple of hundred feet long and they'll see us the minute we get down to that end. They're slow, but they ain't that slow."

"I'll lead them up these stairs," Preacher said. "When they start coming after me, you all head down the stairs at the opposite end and move that barricade."

"You aren't going to be able to hold them off," Granger said.

"I'll be fine," Preacher said. He could barely stand thanks to the pain in his back, but he wasn't going to tell them that. He was their best chance at survival and he knew it. He was sure they knew it too.

"We can't ask you to do that," Granger said.

"You aren't asking, I'm telling you what I'm gonna do," Preacher said. "Now get your ass in gear, you aren't gonna have much time."

Granger nodded.

"You get that van started and wait for me. Swing by and scoop me up as long as I'm not, you know . . . ." He couldn't bring himself to say one of *them*.

Granger nodded again and grabbed Faith's hand. "Come on."

"Junebug, you go on too."

"No fucking way, dipshit," Junebug said. "I ain't leaving you here."

"They need your help moving all that crap we put in front of the door," Preacher said. "Go on and get."

Junebug reached out a hand, grabbed Preacher's shoulder and squeezed. Then he turned away and with Granger and Faith headed to the stairwell that led down to the rear parking entrance.

"We'll pick you up," Granger turned and said. "We won't just leave you."

Preacher nodded and headed in the opposite direction. He could already hear the wheezing moans rising in the stairwell.

## 16.

Granger and Junebug worked fast, keeping Faith out of the way. Granger knew she wanted to help, but she just didn't have the strength needed to move the desks and computers piled in front of the door.

They pushed the items out of the way, placing them in the hallway to slow the approach of the dead at the other end of the hall.

From the moment they reached the bottom of the stairs, the beasts started moving along the hallway toward them, their slow, steady gait bringing them closer and closer. Faith picked up staplers and everything else that was near her and started hurling them at the silhouettes coming toward them. Some of them stopped suddenly and turned back, heading to the stairs at the other end of the hall.

Granger knew that Preacher must have started luring them away, giving them more time. He wanted to believe that the old man would make it out of the building, but he knew the likelihood of that was very slim.

It took less than five minutes to undo the barricade and give themselves enough room to push open the door. It was a straight shot to the vans. Granger felt the cold bite into his skin, invigorating him. They might just make it.

"Come on," he said, starting toward the door.

"I'm going back to give him a hand," Junebug said, heading toward the stairwell door. He tossed the three sets of keys to Granger. "Do like Preacher said, come on back here and pick us up. But if we don't come out after a couple of minutes, I want you to get that little girl someplace safe. And then you don't worry about us no more."

"Hurry," Granger said. "Be careful and get both your asses back here."

"Yup," Junebug said. He took out a cigarette and lit it as he headed into the stairwell.

Granger and Faith started across the parking lot. He scanned from right to left, looking for signs of the dead coming at him through the storm. It was getting hard to see. He reached behind him so Faith could take hold of his hand. She never grabbed it though.

He heard a choking sound.

Granger spun around and saw Castillo with one hand on Faith's throat and his mouth ready to descend on her face.

## 17.

The stairwell was dark and Preacher couldn't see the dead as they crowded through the doorway and started to surge up the stairs. He could hear them though, their low and guttural moans.

He gripped tight his length of iron, waiting for them to come just a bit closer. He could lead them up the stairs, as many of them as possible, and then into one of the rooms with all of the cubicles, keep them occupied for a bit.

He wasn't going to go out without putting up a fight though. As much as it sickened him to do it, he was willing to break more skulls if it meant keeping Junebug and the others alive. He knew this would be his last few minutes alive and his thoughts drifted to his son, wondering if he were safe.

They came up the stairs, clambering over one another to get at him. They fought one another and pushed, each wanting to be the first one to get at Preacher. It slowed them down, and for that, Preacher was thankful.

He backed down the hallway and opened the first door. He reached inside and fumbled for the lights. The overhead fluorescents came on, illuminating the maze of cubicles. The sudden brightness hurt his eyes. He backed all the way into the long room, waiting for the first monster to step inside. The first one through the door wasn't a monster though.

It was Junebug, his face twisting into that wicked pumpkin grin, burning cigarette dangling from his lips. "You didn't think I was gonna leave you all by your lonesome did you?"

"What about the others?"

"They're outside, probably already warming up the van. Let's get our asses out of here before those things all manage to get upstairs."

For a moment, Preacher thought that they just might be able to get away, that they might be able to reach the van ahead of the monsters. The pain in his back didn't seem so bad. Then Cole Jones's massive body lurched through the doorframe behind Junebug and Preacher knew there was not going to be any escape. Cole sniffed the air and seemed to smile.

Before Junebug could even turn around, Cole grabbed him and he sank his teeth down into the side of Junebug's neck. Junebug screamed. It was the most horrible and piteous sound Preacher had ever heard.

Rage coursed through Preacher, giving him strength he hadn't known he had left, made him forget about the pain in his back. He rushed forward and swung the pipe at Cole's skull. The first blow did nothing and Cole continued to chew on screaming Junebug's neck.

The second blow opened up the skull and the third spilled blackened brains. Cole let go of Junebug and fell to the floor.

Junebug dropped to his knees, gurgling through his torn throat as the dead swarmed around him. Preacher raised his pipe again and started swinging as more and more of the dead filled the room.

He didn't stop swinging even as three of the creatures clamped their sharp-toothed mouths onto him and began to feast. The last thing he saw was Holly's face coming toward his.

## 18.

Faith was gasping for air and trying to pull away from Castillo's teeth. One arm hung at Castillo's side, the wrist that Granger had broken when the man was still alive must have rendered it useless even for the dead thing he had become.

Granger rushed forward and slammed the heel of his hand into the side of Castillo's head. He knew it wouldn't hurt Castillo – he was already dead after all. He only hoped to get his attention.

Castillo turned his head, glancing at Granger with his dark eyes but continued to squeeze Faith's throat.

Granger dug into his pocket and pulled out the box cutter. He pulled it open and began slashing at Castillo's face and arms. Though it didn't affect Castillo, it did seem to piss him off.

Castillo batted Granger's hand away, knocking the box cutter loose. He tossed Faith to the ground and turned on Granger. He opened his mouth as though he were trying to say something, but his torn throat was impotent, couldn't make any sound, not even the simple moans of the other dead.

Castillo lunged, his fat body launching into Granger, sending him to the ground. Castillo's good hand was suddenly around Granger's throat, squeezing. Granger tried to push Castillo away, but he was growing weak. He hoped to God that Faith had the good sense just to run away.

Granger knew he was done. He'd lived a violent life and it was only natural that it would come to such a violent end. Faith though, the poor kid had to get away. Granger was only sad that he hadn't been able to keep his promise. He hadn't been able to watch out for her. His eyes closed, blinked, watching the world become fuzzy as he started to lose consciousness.

Above him, and just beyond Castillo's body, was an angel silhouetted in the orange glow of a streetlamp.

She was just a little thing.

She bent forward and Granger could see that the angel was wearing a Jesus Saves t-shirt and she looked pissed off.

Faith jammed the length of the box cutter through Castillo's eye socket and drove it deep into his brain. The fat man shuddered as though he were having a seizure and then stopped moving.

The hand relaxed its grip on Granger's throat, and then Castillo collapsed. Granger had to roll Castillo off him for the second time that night. Better than the alternative though.

Granger sat up and hauled himself to his feet. The other dead were starting to come out of the building now. He saw Junebug and Preacher among them. He and Faith didn't have much time.

Faith sank into Granger's arms and began to cry. After everything that poor girl had been through it was a wonder it took her this long to start crying.

"Come on," he said, ushering her into the first van when he'd found the right set of keys. He locked the doors, started the van, and took off out of the parking lot as the dead began to gather.

The tank was almost full, and even though he wasn't sure where he and Faith were going, he knew that it was better than where either of them had been.

# THE WAY IT GOES

*A soft push from behind . . . blindfolded, I stumble forward and try to right myself.*

I remember when I was a young boy, not more than eight or nine years old, I would go fishing with my father. He would pull fish out of the old millpond behind the house with the pole Momma gave him for his birthday years before. Poppa would pull the fish out of their home, tear the hooks from their gasping mouths, and then snap their backs to stop them from flopping around.

I would stare at their dead, black eyes circled in gold and think how horrible it was to kill them like that. I asked him why we did it.

"Because the greater creature devours the lesser," he said. "That was the way God intended it, and that is the way it will always be."

*I shuffle forward with the others, the stench of sweat and fear filling my nostrils*

Poppa would cut off their heads and slice open their white bellies. Sometimes the girl fish would have eggs in them, and I always felt bad for the babies. I

204

even cried for them sometimes, but Poppa would tousle my hair and tell me, "Kid, don't worry about them. They are less than us."

*I hear a sob arise from in front of me. Someone is calling to a child.*

After gutting them and washing their bodies, he would wrap all but two in cellophane and put them in the freezer. The two that remained were our lunch, and he would fry them in a pan until their skin sizzled and the smell permeated the whole downstairs.

*I can feel the panic growing around me. The time is near.*

Whenever I would eat the fish with my father, I would drown mine in ketchup. It helped to mask the taste of flesh and helped me to forget that the creature on my plate was alive and swimming less than an hour before.

*Someone in front of me tries to run. He pushes past me, but they grab him.*

After our meal, we would retire to the back porch that overlooked the pond. He had a beer, me a soda. The water was usually calm, but sometimes there were ducks. They would paddle around and then dip their heads below the surface to chase some tasty morsel. Poppa said they reminded him of kids bobbing for apples on Halloween. I laughed and burped; the taste of flesh surfaced in my mouth

*Moist hands fumble with my blindfold, removing it. I am in a food factory, just as I knew I would be. The creatures that came to this world a few months ago – I don't remember their proper name – push us toward the spinning blades.*

I remember those lazy days with Poppa, fishing and watching the sun dip behind the mountains. I wouldn't stop asking questions about the poor fish, but he never grew tired of answering. He would always say, "Kid, it's because . . ."

*The greater creature devours the lesser. That is just the way it goes.*

Jason M. Tucker

# F'ROM THE AUTHOR

October 31st, 2009
San Diego, California

Thank you so much for reading this collection of stories. I hope that you've enjoyed reading them as much as I enjoyed writing them. Some of the older stories in this collection that had seen previous publication have been slightly rewritten and updated. If you would like to find out more information about me and about new projects that I'm working on you can visit my website at www.jasonmtucker.com.

As a little something extra, I thought I would include a bit of information about each of the stories, some behind the scenes type stuff that you may (or may not) find interesting. Make sure that you read the stories before you read this section. I don't want you to see something here that might spoil a story for you.

Okay, are you ready? Here we go in no particular order . . .

## "MEAT CITY"

We're all just meat. To the assassin, people are meat with a price, and to the pedophile, people are meat for a terrible purpose. "Meat City" is a zombie story, plain and simple. I dig these kinds of stories; the survival-horror aspect of it all is fun. I enjoy imagining how people from different backgrounds would handle a situation like this.

Granger Black is an important character. He is alluded to in "Ballad of the Pale Rider", which also mentions the Fall of Chicago. I'd love to be able to bridge the gap between the stories someday, to tell about the reason behind the zombies, and to tell about the first of the Riders. We'll see . . . .

## "BALLAD OF THE PALE RIDERS"

Zombies, rifles, cannibals, and frontier heroes in a post apocalyptic landscape are all things that are very near and dear to my heart. I thought that I would smash them all together for a zombie style western, but as I was writing the story I realized that the zombies (while the cause of world ruination) were secondary to the people trying to survive in the outlands and the Pale Riders that protect them. I would like to write more set in this world – it has the potential to go off in many strange directions, and there is all that time between "Meat City" and "Ballad of the Pale Riders" that is full of stories.

## "BAD GIRL"

Long ago, when I was in East San Diego, I lived not too far from a place like The Center in this story. The rehab center was a place where people could go to find help from all manner of problems and addictions, and I met several people who worked there and some who were staying there. Most of them had sad stories, though none had done anything as horrific as Angie had. I don't think the place had any ghosts running around either, but I could be wrong.

Jason M. Tucker

## "CITY OF A MILLION GODS"

The way a religion grows and develops is fascinating, starting with a few fervent believers and then either blossoming or rotting away into obscurity and cult status. This story looks briefly at the beginnings of one such religion and the very first disciples of Bone Dancer, the amalgam of dead gods that came before him. More importantly, to me at least, is the main character who is searching for something in which to believe, even though it's not something that most normal folks would want. (First appeared in *Black Petals* in 2008)

## "CONFESSION OF A RIGHTEOUS SERIAL KILLER"

A recurring aspect in many of my stories is that "those who harm a child will have the pain they caused revisited upon themselves a thousand fold". To me, nothing is more horrifying and sickening than a person who hurts a child. The real world is a harsh place, far more rotten than anything a writer of fiction can put to paper. Revenge is not usually an option. Thankfully, I can remedy that in the stories I tell. (First appeared in *Black Petals* in 1999)

## "COVENTRY GREENS", "RAVEN'S HOUSE", AND "LURES: A FISH STORY"

These stories are from the *Northern Haunts* anthology edited by Tim Deal. All of the locations in these stories are real places – you can look them up on a map to see where the fictional action takes place. Otter Creek, from "Lures" is real, and it empties into Lake Champlain. Hollister Hill Road and the trees beyond exist in real life as well as in "Raven's House". Both Otter Creek and Hollister Hill Road are in Vermont. Harkney Hill Road and Johnson Pond from "Coventry Greens" are real places as well. Go ahead and look them up on a map, maybe even visit them if you are in the area. The stories are made up . . . honest. Just make sure to look over your shoulder occasionally if you head to those areas.

Also, Hooper Johns shares the last name of Thomas from "Ballad of the Pale Riders", and this is not an accident. I hope that I will be able to explore that lineage further someday. (First appeared in *Northern Haunts* in 2009)

## "DOWN IN BACK"

I grew up in northern New York, and on my maternal grandparent's property was a little old dirt road all overgrown with weeds that led to a place we called "Down in Back." When I left home at seventeen, I didn't look back. I was too immature at the time to honor anyone or care about much of anything except myself. I think this story is a reflection of the fear I feel about going back after so many years. I feel it as much now as when I wrote it so many years ago. (First appeared in *Crossroads*, 1999)

## "GOD OF WORMS"

I don't know where the God of Worms came from, and I don't know his plans for the world. I do know that he isn't alone, that there are others out there like him, and others that are far worse. The God of Worms might show up in another story at some point.

## "JUNK BOX"

Almost everyone I know has a junk box, a place where things you thought lost reappear. It might be a kitchen drawer or a box in the attic. I thought it would be interesting if someone started to find other things in the box, things that came back a bit damaged, not quite the same as when they vanished. (First appeared in *Yellow Mama*, 2008)

## "LAST MAGIC"

Everyone in life experiences loss. The pain of losing someone, through death or distance, is a constant that crosses generations, crosses sexes, and crosses races. It would be nice to find a way to make that pain go away.

## "NIGHT FEEDERS"

When I was younger, my father would sometimes wake me up to go ice fishing. Most of the time I would have rather stayed home and eaten pancakes while watching The Smurfs and Scooby-Doo. It was cold out there, bitter. Still, I would usually go, and this story was born of those mornings . . . and my fear of Nazi fish.

## "ORNAMENTS"

A lot of hidden places exist in Southern California, places just out of sight of the highways and the developments, just beyond the safety of the suburbs. The Junkyard might not exist (at leas I haven't found it), but people like Paul, people who are looking for a quick and easy buck, certainly do. Nothing in life comes easy though, and everything has a price. (First Appeared in *The Rare Anthology* 2001)

## "THE DEAD DON'T"

Many years ago, I was able to witness an autopsy and the images from that day (along with the smell) stuck with me. The initial idea of the story came from a dream that I had a short time after viewing the autopsy. In the dream, I woke up and found that I had an autopsy incision. Not the most pleasant dream I'd ever had, but at least I came out of it with a story. (First appeared in *Flashes in the Dark*, 2009)

## "THE PATCHWORK BOY"

This story takes place in the small town of Silver Point, a fictional amalgam of small towns I remember from growing up in Upstate New York. The town shows up in several of my stories. Many strange and horrible things happen in this town; the wandering Mr. Gray and his Frankenstein-magic are just one element. I wonder if Mr. Gray knows anything about the God of Worms . . . .

## "THE WAY IT GOES"

I grew up with a family that fished and hunted. It wasn't for sport; it was for food. We weren't a wealthy family by any means, and if you could catch a few fish that would save on the cost of a meal, you did it. If you could hunt a deer that would provide meat through the winter, you did it. We understood that the greater creature devoured the less because, well, the title says it all. But there is always someone or something out there that is "greater". It's just a matter of time before it shows up with an appetite. (First appeared in *Flashes in the Dark*, 2009)

# ABOUT THE AUTHOR

Jason M. Tucker grew up in the Adirondacks, and he is now a fulltime writer living in Southern California, where the sun always shines and the only thing rising faster than the undead is the cost of living. He's a proud father of two with a (usually) pleasant ex-wife, great ex-girlfriends and an estranged boxer dog named Ember. If he weren't writing, he'd probably be raising and breeding ball pythons. Seriously.

Check out www.jasonmtucker.com to find out more about what he's up to and where you can find other works.

## Staplegun Logic: More Inhuman Resources   by K.K.
### 978-0-9822530-6-9

You've just won a month's stay at the world's most futuristic hotel. Everything's included, except for exits...and food. Well, there's always your fellow guests... You've been locked up in a madhouse for murdering your wife. Only you know that your 'fantasy girls' killed her, and they're only real when they want to be... You're too old to live, too scared to die? No problem! The Recyclers will make you a new body. Just make sure you read the fine print on the warranty... And over THIRTY new worlds of MAYHEM await you From the Author of CLOWNWHITE & INHUMAN RESOURCES!

## The Butcher Bride   by Vince Churchill
### 978-0-9842136-4-1

Thirty years ago, a depraved assault during a Halloween costume ball shattered a young woman's mind, turning her into a brutal mass murderer. Dressed in her rival's blood soaked wedding gown, the legend of the Butcher Bride was born. Now, decades later, everyone who enters the Silas Mansion will discover a frightening spirit ravenous to satisfy perverse appetites.  Death is the only escape.  Here comes the Bride.

## Demon Revolver  by Jason Gehlert   978-0-9822530-7-6

Jason Gehlert offers three terrifying tales of bone-crushing mayhem, blood soaked screams, and demons around every corner. In his first short story collection, Gehlert pulls no punches, delivering on a wide spectrum of genres. The horror western "Revolver," the gritty sequel "Woodsman 2," and the macabre fantasy tale, "Ghost Bride."

## The Gentle Art of Making Enemies   by Kevin Mellor
### 978-0-9822530-7-6

The story behind one of the most ghoulish murder sprees ever carried out-- told first-hand by the killers themselves. By daylight, three Midwestern college students are just anonymous faces in a backpack-sporting crowd. By moonlight, they're responsible for some of the ghastliest crimes in American history. To them it's a joke. For the campus and surrounding town, it's a nightmare. And for anyone who crosses them, it's a crash-course in... The Gentle Art of Making Enemies Class isn't just something to cut... it's something to die for.

## Grave Whispers   by Ryan B. Clark   978-0-9822530-1-4

A girl, pushed by a voice nobody can explain, falls in love with a quiet artist hiding a secret in his attic...a ghost, a succubus, a rogue vigilante, and a boy - the artist, the innocent, the puppet – All together entangled in a bizarre story of love, death, and power from beyond the grave....from beyond the GraveWhispers.....

## Blood Bar  by Norm Applegate   978-0-9822530-1-4

Vampires don't exist....yet, on the brownstone back alley side streets of New York, a vampire dies. Desperate, his lover turns to Kim Bennett, who finds herself caught between a secret vampire society's attempts to locate The Black Testament (a sacred document written by Jack the Ripper) and the modern-day vampire hunters bent on their destruction.

## The Last Church by Lee Pletzers    978-09842136-2-7

The Welcome to Opera Sands. Rachael is a university student studying archeology. On her latest dig, her team enters a slip in time and arrives 3 months after Peter –an antique dealer who sold his soul for the Devil's Wish Book- dies. He leaves behind a supernatural dagger, a dagger which houses his destructive soul. Upon its discovery, she accidentally cuts herself. The end of the world is at hand, unless evil is defeated within the holy grounds of The Last Church.

## The Everborn: Special Edition   by Nicholas Grabowsky
### 978-0-9842136-0-3

*The Everborn* concerns the offspring of fallen angels that have lived among us since the dawn of man. Throughout the ages, they live life after life in normal society until each one falls in love and fathers their own child. Before that child is born, they undergo a rapid degeneration into a fetal state before they disappear entirely and become reborn into a new life. When an Everborn is reborn as a set of twins, one a soulless serial killer on a quest to be born again into a sinless life and the other a kind-hearted ghostwriter for a world-famous rock-and-roll horror novelist, a banished Watchmaid claims her role in an ancient prophecy to use the soulless twin as a means to re-enter our world and bring about its destruction.

## Holiday Madness    by Fred Wiehe
### 978-0-9842136-5-8

13 Dark Tales for Halloween, Christmas, and All Occasions The holidays have never before been more spine-tingling or more fun for Tweens, Teens, and Adults alike than in this anthology of 13 supernatural tales.

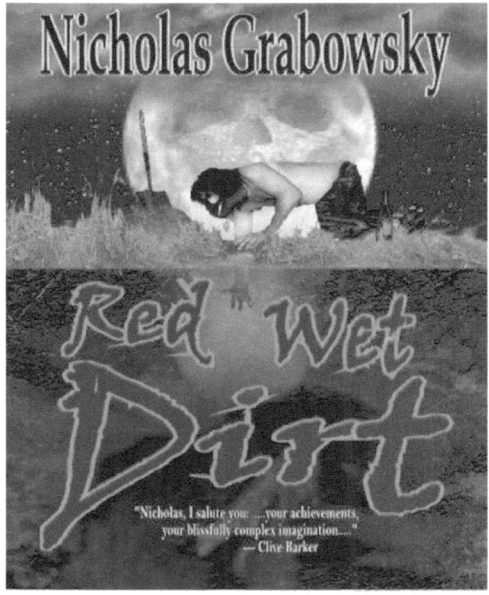

## Blood Orchard   by S.D. Hintz   978-0-9842136-7-2

Francine Heller fantasizes about prom dresses and romantic dances. Three bullies butcher her dreams into nightmares. When she is beaten and left for dead, vengeance bleeds from the town orchard to a barn of bottled screams.   Coren's panic room is a haunted tomb. And the more secrets he unearths, the more evidence there is to hide from a sheriff hell-bent on framing him.

## Chophouse   by Horns   978-0-9842136-8-9

A sinister night falls over the relaxed rural community of Dominic County. Before the light of day would return to the quiet woodland town, many came to believe that the gates of Hell had broken open and the Devil's minions were rampantly spreading terror and death there. The Chophouse is OPEN!

## Human Nature   by Matthew Ewald   978-0-9842136-6-5

The only survivor of the grisly aftermath of an activist raid on an animal testing lab leaves him institutionalized. When his psychiatrist begins to unlock the secrets to the events of that fateful night, she finds it is up to the both of them to stop the unspeakable evil that was unleashed upon the world.

Look for
us
wherever
books
are sold.